# CLAYTON STONE,
## Facing Off

### ENA JONES

Holiday House / New York

Printed and bound in July 2016 at Maple Press, York, PA, USA.
www.holidayhouse.com
First Edition
1 3 5 7 9 10 8 6 4 2
Library of Congress Cataloging-in-Publication Data
Names: Jones, Ena, author.
Title: Clayton Stone, facing off / by Ena Jones.
Description: First edition. | New York : Holiday House, [2016] | Sequel to:
Clayton Stone, at your sevice. | Summary: "Middle-school spy Clayton Stone
goes undercover to protect the President's son, attending a new school and
playing lacrosse against his real friends and former teammates"—Provided
by publisher.
Identifiers: LCCN 2016000934 | ISBN 9780823436484 (hardcover)
Subjects: | CYAC: Spies—Fiction. | Presidents—Family—Fiction. |
Lacrosse—Fiction. | Boarding schools—Fiction. | Schools—Fiction.
Classification: LCC PZ7.1.J68 Cm 2016 | DDC [Fic]—dc23 LC record available at
https://lccn.loc.gov/2016000934

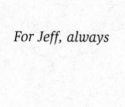

*For Jeff, always*

# 1

The back of Kyle Hampton's head pushes hard against my mouth, and I realize this is probably not how we should have been introduced.

Yup. My assignment is going really well. I've just tackled the president's kid and shoved him into a toilet stall. As in, the son of the president of the United States. As in, a *toilet* stall.

I didn't have a choice! I've been a student at the Sydney Brown Middle School less than fourteen minutes; the door with the FACULTY BATHROOM sign was the only logical option. Where the heck else could I hole up with him?

It's practically impossible to get my SpiPhone and keep hold of Kyle—Captain Thompson did warn me this job might get complicated—and now it sounds like a sledgehammer is coming through the bathroom door. I need help, preferably within the next thirty seconds.

How did I get into this mess, just when I thought life had returned to normal?

It started with an abrupt knock on my thigh—the Special Service version of a text.

# 2

Friday, just before noon—

I'm sucking down the usual sausage pizza, fruit mish-mash and chocolate milk, trading play-off talk with my lacrosse teammates. We're scattered across two side-by-side tables in the back of Masters Academy cafeteria.

The final game of the season is next Wednesday, when we go against the number one team in our division: Sydney Brown. Percy saw their last game and came back with a full report. He said they're good, but the worst news is they've got a maniac on their team, number 23, who's famous for sending guys to the sidelines and, apparently, one time to the hospital.

It'll be tough, but if we win against SB, we're practically guaranteed a spot in the second round of regional play-offs. If we lose, it's a shot in the dark.

The entire team's agreed that there's only one thing to do: win.

My best friend, Toby, is inhaling a hot dog while I relax into another bite of pizza. My eyes drift to the next table and I notice Laci Peters smiling at me. I smile back, because we're sort of friends now. Plus, Toby has a serious thing for her.

Besides the new SpiPhone in my pocket and my weird friendship with Laci, life is pretty much back to normal. It definitely wasn't normal a few weeks ago when I helped the Special Service capture a ring of kidnappers who targeted malls; now they're all in jail waiting for their big trial.

Except for the short patches of hair sprouting from my teammates' heads—which they shaved to protect *me*—it's like the whole mall napper thing never happened. Not one of them has mentioned it. Every so often, one of the guys rubs his fuzz-top and grins. But that's it. They know my identity has to remain secret—top secret—if I'm gonna keep helping the Special Service. And that's what I call true brothers. I've got twenty-four of them.

I've wondered when the Special Service will need me again, so when my SpiPhone knocks like a gavel against my leg, a tingle runs up my spine. I reach into my pocket and clasp the phone, hoping I'm not imagining things. It thumps again, and I bite down my grin. I gotta go read whatever text just showed up—in private.

Headmistress Templeton and Captain Thompson agreed, after Gran bullied them into it, that I should have custody of my Special Service SpiPhone full-time. It's kind of cool because Agent Jones worked some of his technology magic and now the phone has two numbers: my old "regular" number, and my new Special Service number. He even trained me to recognize the coded rings and vibrations so I immediately know which number is being used and how quickly I need to grab a hall pass.

"Where ya going, Clayton?" says Toby, his eyes alert as he watches me straddle the bench and pick up my tray.

The words aren't out of Toby's mouth before I've got ten sets of eyes pretending not to care about me ducking out with half-eaten pizza on my plate—something I've done, uh, *never*.

Until now.

I return Toby's gaze and shrug. "When ya gotta go, ya gotta go" is all I can think to say.

And then I about-face and head to the cafeteria doors, knowing he won't keep asking this time. I grab the Spi-Phone from my pocket as I hit the hallway and jog to the nearest stairwell. Looking both ways, I slip behind the stairs and stand in the light of the window. I type the first password and then press my thumb to the screen to make it through the next security wall. Finally, the Special Service icons pop up.

The text widget is flashing the number 2, but considering I've never received a text on this side of the "wall," I'm not sure that's normal.

I press it, and the messages appear. They're from my grandmother.

**Liza Stone**
**Today 12:07 PM**
**Go to front of M Academy ASAP.**
**Cpt is waiting.**

Leave? Without telling anybody? In the middle of a school day? Can I *do* that?

I reread Gran's texts: **ASAP. Waiting.**

I think that means *N-O-W.*

My phone reads 12:10 p.m., only a few minutes before the bell rings and lunch is over. Maybe I should wait so

I can get lost in the crowded halls as I sneak out. I look down at the messages again.

They're gone.

I press at the screen, but it's no use. The texts aren't there anymore.

I poke my head into the hallway and look both ways. Some kid is at his locker, too far away for me to tell who it is.

The heck with it. I sprint down the hall about twenty yards, around the corner, another fifteen strides and through the main atrium and out the heavy door that leads outside. I know the security cameras will catch me, but maybe I'll luck out and nobody will be paying attention. The school secretary has to eat, too, and she's the one who usually monitors the entrance.

My feet carry me down the steps, and I register the screech of fast tires turning the corner a block away. There's a gleaming black Suburban speeding toward me. It comes to a perfectly timed stop at the precise moment my shoe touches the curb, and the back door pops open.

Gran has always warned me not to get into a car with strangers, but I don't check before I hop inside. I close the door, grab the seat belt and make myself comfortable.

Up front, a suit is driving. I turn to Captain Thompson, who's staring at me from the next seat over, his arm still in a sling.

My fault.

"I want you to know I threw away a perfectly good piece of pizza for you."

His response is trigger quick. "Don't worry, Clayton. Plenty of pizza to come. As of this weekend, you're moving in with me—and I don't cook."

# 3

I've got a gazillion questions, but Captain Thompson's been on his cell phone since the second he told me I'm gonna be living with him, so I've only gotten one answer: his forehead squeeze that says *Not now.*

After a twelve-minute drive the suit stops the Suburban deep inside the parking garage of the Special Service building. We step out of the SUV into the shadows, and the captain takes three strides to a solid gray door, where he presses his finger to a barely visible piece of metal. The door unlocks with a series of clicks, and we enter through a hallway. We reach the main area, which is airplane-hangar huge. It's lined with computer panels and screens on one level, and floor-to-ceiling maps of the United States and the rest of the world that flash information like current weather and air traffic on the next. Higher still, there are ginormous flat-screens set to news channels all over the world.

I'm still in awe of the place, and as I scan the enormous room the flashbacks kick in: ducking out of school after Laci told me her friend Amber Meldon was in trouble;

convincing Carlos to help me; failing to convince Gran's assistant, Frankie, to help me; ~~stealing~~ borrowing a Special Service car and driving it to the mall nappers' house.

It was Friday, April thirteenth. My thirteenth birthday. The day I got kidnapped on purpose so I could help Amber and her mom escape from the mall nappers—who were going to murder them.

I follow Captain Thompson through the hub of Special Service headquarters and wonder what kind of trouble I'm going to get myself into this time. It's killing me not to ask.

As we cross the main office area, I notice that the wall to Gran's office is open. Up until a few weeks ago, I thought the only thing different about my grandmother was that she owns Big Stone's Diner and loves pickles as much as my grandfather hated them—when he was alive.

We enter her office and I sit where the captain points, at the slick black conference table, and look around. The glossy photos, Gran's supersized desk, the American flag. It's still hard for me to believe she's in charge of all this: *Chief* Liza Stone, Head of the Special Service. There's a stack of files on her desk and, on the floor beside it, a couple of suitcases and my backpack, computer bag and lacrosse gear.

So the move is happening now. As in, right now.

Captain Thompson finally pokes the screen on his phone and awkwardly returns it to his holster. Even though he's right-handed and the sling holds his left arm, I guess it's difficult to do stuff with one hand. As he fumbles, his suit jacket is pushed back and I see the strap for another holster—and his gun.

I wonder how hard it will be for him if he needs to use *that*.

Another reminder: my fault.

I'm opening my mouth to speak when Gran comes whisking into the room from the back corridor. She's got a black duffel bag strapped over her shoulder and is wheeling a small suitcase. Her smile is aimed straight at me until she notices Captain Thompson.

"Oh, good! You're back," she says, immediately changing direction. She hands the bag to the captain.

He takes it and hoists it up and down, testing its weight. "What's this?"

"A few gadgets for my amusement, and one or two things for Clayton." Then she gestures to a laptop sitting open on the conference table. "Have you got everything else ready?"

I'm about to ask *What gadgets?* but it's too late. They've already rolled into an intense, eyeball-to-eyeball discussion about the "cover" house: the security regimen, whether they should install more cameras, potential defense strategies and when it was last swept for bugs and other devices. "That house needs to be secure, top to bottom," says Gran. She points to her suitcase. "I've decided you and Clayton need a maid. You have no idea how difficult it is to keep up with the laundry of an athletic young man."

Captain Thompson laughs. "When was the last time you did laundry? I'll take fine care of Clayton."

"Maybe," Gran says with a small shrug. "But he's my only grandson, and if he's there, I'm there."

Captain Thompson is silent for a moment before he folds. "Okay, Liza. You win."

There's only one way they're going to include me in this conversation, so I dive in headfirst. "Anybody planning to tell me what's going on? I'm missing a very important pre-algebra class, ya know. There's a test Monday."

Both heads snap in my direction.

"Oh, Clayton!" says Gran, holding out her arms and coming in for a hug. "I'm sorry. Usually I don't get so deeply involved in setting up a cover house. But since my favorite grandson will be living there, I want to personally make sure everything is in order."

I skip the usual reminder that I'm her *only* grandson. "So you're not talking about Captain T's house?"

"No." She sits beside me at the conference table and points to the pile of files on her desk. "Derek, will you bring those over so we can explain matters to Clayton?"

Finally. "Did something happen?"

Captain Thompson sits across from us, keeps two folders and pushes the rest across the table to Gran—with his good hand. "Okay, Clayton," he says. "Let's start with the basics."

The captain opens the top file and shows me a picture of a boy my age. I recognize him immediately. Anybody would; it's Kyle Hampton, the son of President Hampton, the second African-American president in the history of the United States.

I lean in, my heart pumping a little faster, remembering when Amber, Senator Meldon's stepdaughter, was kidnapped by the mall nappers. "Is he missing?"

Gran sighs. "Oh, no, dear. Not at all."

Captain Thompson's expression is grim. "But we want to make sure it stays that way. Your grandmother received a call from the president, requesting our assistance. Or, rather, *yours*."

"Mine?"

Both the captain and Gran nod as Gran begins to explain. "Kyle goes to a private school that is, for the most part, one of the most secure campuses in the United States. Several students have their own security personnel, although they aren't as hands-on as Kyle's bodyguards. Despite all the highly trained agents hanging about, Sydney Brown has a problem."

Captain Thompson opens the next file. "This week the school became aware of a computer breach. Hackers stole all the staff, parent and student files, which included home addresses, Social Security numbers and other personal information."

"What does that have to do with Kyle?"

"Nothing, we hope," says Gran. "But we've been alerted to some strange online posts naming Sydney Brown as a target. To make matters worse, there were two recent attempts to bypass school security using the back way, through the woods. Both trespassers claimed they'd lost their way, and one of them was walking a dog, so it's feasible; however, all of this together creates significant concern."

"You're afraid somebody's trying to get to him?"

The captain shrugs. "We're looking into every possibility. There was a lockdown at the school last week because of a mysterious package, and the bomb squad was called. Because of the risk, any unknown package at the school is treated as a threat." He looks at Gran before turning back to me. "There's another small issue. Apparently, Kyle has been acting unusual lately. Quieter, not sharing as much around the dinner table, that sort of thing. The president is worried that something is bothering his son but can't figure out what it could be."

"Has anybody asked Kyle?"

Captain Thompson nods. "Kyle insists nothing is wrong."

Gran taps one of the folders in front of her. "The president has ordered a full investigation at every level. However, there is a gap in the plan, and he's come up with an interesting way to fill it."

Captain Thompson leans forward. "President Hampton's idea is to assign an undercover agent—apart from his regular bodyguards—to stay close to Kyle, even when he's playing sports. This person would covertly befriend and keep track of him." The corner of his mouth turns up, and there's a mischievous light in his eyes as he adds, "Not many people I know could pull that off."

He's right about that.

Oh. Duh. "So—me."

Gran nods. "You impressed the president with your work on the mall nappers case, Clayton, especially the way you helped bring them in." She squeezes my shoulder and our eyes meet. "So he's asked that you enroll at Kyle's school and work undercover, to help protect his son. Hopefully you can figure out why Kyle is acting different lately."

"I'm supposed to go undercover as his friend?" I look over at my stuff piled next to Gran's desk. "It doesn't sound like you're asking me if I want to do this."

No answer.

I try really hard to hold back my groan. "Our last game is Wednesday, and then play-offs start. We may only be in middle school, but do you know how many high school and college coaches watch the final play-off teams? And we could win the title this year."

Captain Thompson grimaces. "I'm glad you brought that up. There's one more thing."

Really? This should be good.

"Since Kyle plays lacrosse, you're going to be playing for Sydney Brown."

O.M.G. How did that not-so-little detail fly over my head? Sydney Brown. *Sydney Brown*.

I feel my forehead hit the table, but I'm not sure how it got there.

Dear God, please don't let this happen.

There's a hand on my shoulder. "Clayton? Are you all right?"

I lift my head and look into my grandmother's eyes. "No. Sydney Brown is the team we play on Wednesday. Tell me how I'm supposed to play against my own team in the most important game of the year. The guys will never forgive me."

Gran's lips are thin and pressed tight as she stares back at me. "We'll figure that out when the time comes," she says after way too long a pause. "For now, you need to get as close to Kyle as you can. If he's at lacrosse practice, you'll be there, too. If he joins the glee club, start humming, because you'll be in the row behind him. By lunch on Monday, you're going to be the best friend he never knew he didn't have."

This time I don't stop the groan. It blows out of my mouth so hard I swear it makes the American flag in the corner sway.

Captain Thompson sends me a stern look. "Clayton, this is important. Are you in?"

"Yeah, right. Have *you* ever figured out how to say no to POTUS?"

Gran laughs in her most unfunny way. "I'm glad you realize what we're up against."

"But you *do* have a choice," says Captain Thompson. "And it's about your attitude. Imagine if your coach sent a player onto the field when they didn't want to play."

*Exactly.*

My insides are going all wackadoo. I swear, I get what the captain's saying. But that doesn't make it any easier to say yes, even when the president is the one calling the shots.

I guess that's the point. The president is calling the shots.

I take a deep breath. "I'll do it."

The captain arches an eyebrow. "One hundred percent?"

I face him, my eyes drawn to his arm, with his fingers dangling out the end of the sling. I know what he's asking.

"Yeah," I say. "A hundred percent."

## Sunday, May 6, 3:00 P.M.

# 4

It's the longest weekend of my life. The Special Service doesn't just rebuild me on the outside, there are three huge binders of background information to memorize while they poke, pull and prod my face. There's even a coach to teach me a new way to walk and talk.

Agent Brick and I have gotten to be good friends. Not.

She tests me every time I make it through a section in the binders. Family history, maps of the school and DC area, teachers and students—and tons of weird stuff. Like, what *not* to say. I don't know how many times I almost fall asleep answering her questions. Nobody should study so hard on a weekend, especially not me.

Then there's Gran's black duffel bag. Other than a couple of snazzy bow ties that must have belonged to my grandfather, there are no cool gadgets for me. No stun pens or sedative sticks, and definitely not her miniature cannon or the superclassified drone.

Jeez. Don't undercover agents need stuff? I start to grumble, but then I come right out and ask. "Not even a stun pen? I'll keep it turned off."

"*No*," she says as she lifts her skirt and secures a laser gun in a holster above her knee. "Not this time."

"Why not?"

"Clayton, you are going to a school. Absolutely no weapons; *nothing* that could identify you as anything other than a typical student."

"What about Kyle's bodyguards? They have weapons."

"That's different."

"Aren't I supposed to protect Kyle?"

"Not like that," she says in a disapproving tone.

There's no use arguing with her, but I honestly think a stun pen might come in handy at a school. She's forgetting one very important fact: it's a *pen*.

"Oh, Clayton," she says with a chuckle, "don't look so downhearted." She digs in her bag and hands me a small padded pouch. "Here are a couple of video cameras we're testing out. They work with an app that's already been loaded on your phone. Who knows? Maybe you'll find a use for them."

I lift the practically weightless pouch. "Thanks," I say, totally not feeling the love.

"One more thing, and it's vital," she says. "After much deliberation, the president has decided not to tell Kyle's security detail about you. He thinks doing so would jeopardize the entire effort, and perhaps future assignments."

I open my mouth to speak, but Gran interrupts straight-away. "I know, this may put you in a more challenging position if there is a crisis. But the president is in charge. His son, his decision."

No pen, and no backup; practically naked. At least I get to keep my SpiPhone.

By the time Monday morning arrives, my brain needs a break and the trip to Sydney Brown Middle School feels like a vacation. For a whole ten minutes I'm by myself in a Mercedes stretch limo.

I flip open the megasized vanity mirror and stare hard at the prepped-out brainy kid who meets my eyes, searching for something recognizable. I finally decide on my teeth. They've inserted a temporary implant inside my nose to make it wider, weaved wavy pieces into my dyed hair, and put chocolate-brown contact lenses in my eyes. Add the mandatory yet oh-so-fashionable bow tie, oxford shirt and khakis, and say hello to Max Carrington—the new me.

My look today is also parentless, supposedly like so many other Sydney Brown kids. My "father," Captain Thompson going by the name Mitchell Carrington, is a political consultant, and he's too busy to escort me. My mom died of cancer two years ago, something nobody is supposed to talk about because it upsets me. I don't have to fake that. My real mom is dead, and it *does* upset me. My real dad, too. And Gramps. It's not fair and I hate everything to do with death, and not only do I not want to talk about it, I for sure don't want to think about it.

I stare out the window and concentrate hard on the security gatehouse we've stopped at. The guard might look official, but with only a walkie-talkie strapped to his belt, how serious can he be?

The guard gets us checked in, and the bright yellow arm that separates Sydney Brown from the rest of the world rises and lets us continue up the long drive to the school's horseshoe entrance.

We're kind of late, and the driver, a real Special Service agent, puts the Mercedes in park and gets out. From behind his sunglasses he casts a casual glance around us, probably noticing every detail. He moves like a mountain lion around the car, and I can tell he's ready to spring in any direction, even slide under the limo, with almost no warning. He's ready for the unexpected—he *expects* the unexpected. That's the type of agent I want to be someday.

He opens the trunk, and I hear him shuffle things around as he gets my backpack and lacrosse bag. I've been instructed to stay put until he opens the door for me.

When he does, I see myself in the reflection of his shades as he hands me my stuff. There's a quick "Good luck, kid" from the side of his mouth as I take my first steps toward the school, but when I turn to respond he's already ducked inside the limo.

I hurry up the walkway to find the main office. I think back to one of the building maps Agent Brick gave me, but then see a sign that says ADMINISTRATION, complete with an arrow pointing the way.

I enter the office and come face-to-face with a lady sitting at a desk. She's busy telling a man in a Comcast uniform that she needs him to get the Internet problems fixed for good this time. From what Gran says, they've run new background checks on every single employee or serviceperson who sets foot on school property, just to be safe. But I look them both over anyway. I *am* working undercover.

The lady immediately stands and smiles when she sees me. "You must be Max," she says, walking around the desk and the cable guy to greet me. "We don't usually get new students toward the end of the year, but we're glad to have you at Sydney Brown."

I put out my hand and we shake. "Good to be here."

"Your father called to say you'd be late, but don't worry. It's a little crazy around here this morning. Our computer system is down again." She turns to the cable man and asks, "Do you know where you're going?" But he's not listening to her. He's staring at me from underneath his wide-brimmed Comcast cap.

"New, huh?" he says. "That's tough at your age. Where'd you come from?"

It takes a second for me to remember. "Uh, a town outside Chicago."

The lady walks to the door and opens it. "We really need our system up and running."

The man winks at me, then nods and tugs at the brim of his cap as he walks out the door. "No worries, you'll be back online in a heartbeat," he says. "I'm the best around."

She exhales loudly as the door closes behind him, like she's glad he's gone. Then she returns to her desk, picks up a manila envelope and hands it to me. "This is your schedule, your locker number and a map of the school." I put down my lacrosse gear and start to open the envelope, but she bends down to pick up a black nylon bag beside her desk and hands that to me, too. "This is your tablet. It has most of your class texts, teacher websites—practically everything—loaded on it. And if that gentleman can get us back online for more than five minutes, you'll find it very useful."

"Thanks," I say, throwing the computer bag's strap over my shoulder.

Her hand is out again. "And here's your student ID. We used your application photo, but it's easy to change if you'd like. You'll need it for any purchases on campus and to get into school events." She glances to her right and frowns before returning her attention to me. "I know you're supposed to meet Headmistress Williams, but something has come up, and I'm afraid that won't be possible this morning. I'm sure she'll catch up with you as soon as she can."

I look at the closed door only a few feet away. There's a gold nameplate that says HEADMISTRESS GERALDINE WILLIAMS.

Next thing I know, the secretary's heading past me into the hallway. I pick up my gear and catch up just as she points down the hall. "Take the first left, then right, and then left again. Your locker will be on the left. And your first class, which has already begun, is a little farther up the same hallway. Any questions?"

Yeah. Can I skip my first class?

"No, thanks. I'll be okay."

"Great. Have a good day. I'll try to check in with you later."

I glance back at the nameplate on her desk, kicking myself for not noticing earlier. "Thanks, Ms. Hernandez."

She pats me on the back, and this time her smile seems brighter. "You're welcome, Max."

I tuck my student ID into my pocket and pad down the carpeted hallway, trying not to rock my shoulders when I walk, something I never realized I did before I had five agents staring me down, pointing out everything from the way I raise my right eyebrow when I ask a question, to the way it sounds like "bull" when I say "bowl," and apparently the unique way I lumber as I travel from Point A to Point Z.

The carpet makes it feel like I'm in some sort of hotel,

not a school. I turn left, passing classroom doors every twenty feet or so, and then right. Tall, wide lockers that alternate the school colors, black and gold, run the length of this hallway. Pretty cool.

By the time I turn again, starting to count down the numbers to my locker, I'm loving the feel of this place. There are nooks with couches and reclining chairs that look comfortable enough to sleep on, and charging stations like you see in some airports. Instead of regular water fountains, there are water coolers with big jugs, and spigots for cold and hot water, and I swear I smell coffee beans, as if there's a Starbucks around the corner.

Oh, yeah. No matter what this school looks like, it stinks because Toby's not here. And neither is the mocha he usually brings me from his father's coffee shop.

I stare up at my locker, 1115, and pull the paper Ms. Hernandez gave me out of my pocket. I'm guessing all I'll need is the envelope and the leather bag with my new tablet, so I put the rest inside my locker, which is so big there's even room for my lacrosse gear.

I stare at my schedule, knowing I'll probably be walking into the middle of the teacher's lecture, the worst possible way for a new kid to make an entrance. Plus, Kyle will be there.

I turn and start in the direction of my highly anticipated Advanced World History class. For half a second I consider staking out Kyle's locker—it's across the hall and down a few—but then two things happen simultaneously.

#1: A giant man in the standard dark-suit-and-earpiece getup comes whizzing around the corner, his eyes on full alert. #2: The emergency lights start flashing along with a pulsing, high-pitched tone.

The man positions himself directly in front of the set of lockers where Kyle's should be, as kids begin pouring into the hallway. I look him up and down and then I see it, on the floor, between the agent's feet. A sealed brown package, about the size of a large shoe box. And the way the agent is standing over it, he definitely doesn't want anybody near it.

Could it be a—

Holy mother of ticking time bombs. *Now?*

Kids are scrambling all around me. A voice comes through the speakers, breaking into the shrill alarm: "Code Number Two Lockdown! Go immediately to your assigned safe zone!"

I don't know what a Code Number Two Lockdown is, but from the way people are moving, and the look of the agent towering over that mystery box, I have a pretty good guess.

The captain says the point of all this security is to protect Kyle a hundred percent, even if the risk turns out to be zero, because there are no do-overs, something Kyle probably doesn't understand. Can't blame him, though. Until recently, I didn't, either.

There's only one thing to do: find Kyle Hampton and keep him the heck away from here—until this lockdown is over.

## MONDaY, MaY 7, 8:27 a.m.

# 5

For a split second my brain is turned around, trying to figure out which way to go. World History is farther up the hallway on the left, and Kyle should be heading with the crowd, which would take him directly past his locker.

Dang it! All the warnings from this weekend come back, crisscrossing through my brain. Agent Brick kept telling me that my job is to blend in, but I can't let Kyle come this way. I've got to intercept him. Gran says they've spotted strangers hanging around, and that box the agent's guarding had to come from somewhere. Even if there's only a 0.1 percent chance that it's a bomb, I've got to react as if the threat is 100 percent real. Just like Captain Thompson says.

I fight my way upstream, against the flow of students who seem to know exactly where they're going, scanning the faces for Kyle's. *Where is he?*

As I move past his locker I stop and glance over at the bodyguard. Everyone else is giving him a wide berth, like they know he's not somebody to mess with. I hesitate a moment too long; his Frankenstein arm stretches three feet across and his hand lands on my shoulder like a piece of granite. "Get going, kid. You can't stay here."

I want to explain who I am, that I'm here to help—only, I can't.

I slip from underneath his hold and plunge back in, moving against the sea of students heading to their assigned safe zones. Less than thirty seconds later, the huge number of kids has thinned out, and my heart begins to race. Maybe I missed him.

But then I spot a kid at the far end of the hall, doing something on his phone. When he looks up, his eyes are on me. He's a black kid, with tightly cropped hair, and I know it's Kyle. Not because of his skin or hair, but because of the way he's standing. He's putting off attitude that hits me strong from twenty yards away—it says, *We just had one of these stupid lockdowns last week. I'm not going anywhere.* I'm guessing it takes presidential DNA to have attitude like that.

It's obvious he's ready to bolt, so I slow down and pretend to read locker numbers, not that that makes any sense. The lights are flashing and long, urgent sirens are piercing the air. What idiot's gonna visit their locker at a time like this?

But I don't know what else to do, so I keep moving. As I get closer I take a quick glimpse and realize he's sizing me up.

His eyes return to his phone. He's deciding what to do. By now we must be the only ones in the hallway, but at about five yards away, I glance back.

There are two people where the halls intersect, and they're running toward us. Fast. The guy taking the rear looks like that agent from Kyle's locker, and I think he's chasing somebody. Whoever he's after is a lot shorter than the Superman-sized agent. A kid? But what kid would run from Kyle's bodyguard?

It's impossible to think with all this noise. I've got to get Kyle somewhere safe, locked down and away from *them* and whatever else is happening.

When I turn back to Kyle, the expression on his face has changed. I know that look—it's a *Where the heck did the ball go?* when you've lost it on the lacrosse field. He's confused. But there's no time to explain.

A few feet beyond him I see a sign for a faculty bathroom. So much for "blending in" and becoming friends first. I let the envelope and leather computer bag slip to the floor and swoop forward the last two steps, extending my arm while I yell over the blaring alarm, "We gotta go!"

Kyle's eyes widen as I'm about to plunge into him, and he opens his mouth to speak, but no words come out. I wrap my arm around his shoulders and, using all my momentum, pull him across the hall and through the bathroom door.

I shove him as far into the bathroom as I can, force the door the rest of the way shut and throw the bolt.

We're locked in, and the noise is muted, but maybe it's not enough.

I don't know what's going to happen next. Lockdowns are serious, especially when a suspicious package is involved. Will they call the bomb squad again? And who was that bodyguard chasing?

I tell myself I've done the right thing. It's not like I can let Kyle run around the school alone—he might walk straight into his own death trap.

Kyle has backed himself against the far wall and is giving me a look like a cornered animal. The dangerous kind.

"Are you crazy? *Do you know who I am?*"

Yeah, I know who he is, and if this is the one-in-a-million time when there's something real going on, like a bomb or a shooter, I've got to get him to the safest possible place. My eyes dart across the room. Under the sinks?

No, not enough protection.

My eyes flit to the left. There are only three stalls, but they're each bricked in, floor to ceiling.

I look back at Kyle. There's a fire in his eyes, but with it, a shadow of doubt.

"We need to take cover," I say, moving toward him again.

He shakes his head, like there's no way he's listening to me. "Stay away from me. I have bodyguards. My father—"

He doesn't understand, so there's only one way to do this. I come at him and tackle him from the side, twisting his body so I can wrap my left arm around his chest. Then I push him forward into the stall at the very end, the one with the most brick.

One way or another, we're taking cover.

He squirms and pushes, doing his best to find a way out of my lock, but somehow I manage to cram both of us inside. I slam the door closed with my hip and try to settle Kyle down by holding him tight. The back of his head knocks hard against my mouth and I get a not-so-great taste of his hair.

Holy mother of toilet water! "Knock it off! What do you think? I'm gonna give you a swirly?"

Yeah. This is definitely not the way we should have been introduced, but there's no going back now.

I can't get to my SpiPhone while the guy is fighting me like this—and it sounds like a sledgehammer is ramming the bathroom door. I need Captain Thompson or *somebody*, preferably within the next thirty seconds.

Crud. Crud. Crud.

I squeeze Kyle harder, and this time it works. He freezes under my grip. The alarms have stopped sounding in the background, but the pounding on the door is still coming strong.

He's got to see that he needs to cooperate for both our sakes. "Listen, I gotta call for help. So I'm gonna let you go, okay?"

"Help? *Help?*" Kyle twists his head, trying to look at me. "*Help* is trying to get in here—to save me from *you*."

And that's when a voice like a megaphone comes through, loud and clear. "This is Federal Agent Jason Kang. Stand back from the door. We're coming in!"

6

What we've got here is a failure to communicate.

Seriously.

How the heck was I supposed to know the box in front of Kyle's locker had his science project inside? And why didn't anybody tell me that Sydney Brown's monthly lockdown drill would be today? Precisely eleven minutes after I blew through the school's doors.

I am sunk like the *Titanic*.

Headmistress Williams's office is cool, though. Plenty of cushy chairs for all the people suddenly interested in the psychologically challenged new kid. They're acting like I *did* give Kyle a swirly. Even the cable man, who's bent over a box behind the headmistress's desk, is paying more attention to the craziness revolving around me than the wires he's supposed to be messing with.

Does this mean I get to go back to Masters?

I'm half listening to the complaints ricocheting back and forth between the adults. Words like *exposure* and *risk* and *new student orientation* are cruising hard and fast—torpedoes, all aimed at me.

Captain Thompson, aka Mitchell Carrington, finally stands and clears his throat. He's practically a different person from last night; the Special Service added blubber to his belly and around his face. They also messed with his hair in a way I bet he's not happy about—he's half bald. And his arm sling is missing. I sure hope his shoulder isn't hurting too much.

"I certainly apologize for Max's mistake. As he's told you, he thought there was a true emergency and was acting in the best interest of the president's son." He pauses and steps to the side of Headmistress Williams's desk as he looks back and forth between the headmistress and Federal Agent Jason Kang. "But I must say, if a member of Kyle's security detail had been with him at the time of the lockdown, none of this would have happened."

Every head in the room swings toward Agent Kang.

"Good point," says the headmistress, her head cocked inquisitively. "Mr. Kang?"

Agent Kang sputters back at her. "Kyle's science project had been delivered and he asked me to secure it. Another agent was on his way. I admit there was a lapse, but—"

After sputtering some more, he finally sits straighter in his chair and leans forward, shaking his head vehemently. This time when he speaks, his tone is accusing and belligerent. "I want to know why this new student's application did not go through regular channels. The entire family is supposed to be vetted through our system before they're admitted. Standard protocol."

The office is drop-dead silent. Agent Kang has obviously asked a question the headmistress does not want to answer, because with all eyes on her, she's twiddling her pen like it's a hot potato.

Finally, she clears her throat. "I received a call requesting that I waive the usual application process in order to bring Max into Sydney Brown immediately." She waves her long fingers in the air and continues. "Mr. Carrington's move here was expedited, and it was a priority to secure his son's admission. I apologize to your agency for not informing you, but I only had a few hours' notice."

Agent Kang turns about five shades of beet juice. "What do you mean, a call? Who has the authority to jeopardize the safety of Kyle Hampton?"

Headmistress Williams finally stops fiddling. She raises her chin defiantly and looks Agent Kang straight in the eyes. "The president of the United States, that's who."

# 7

Now I really do know the fastest—and the worst—way to introduce myself to an entire school: make an enemy of the president's kid, his friends and the federal agent in charge of his security detail.

Brilliant. In other words, stupid.

After the meeting, where somehow they decide I can stay, and a short but definitely uncomfortable—and public—chat with Pops, during which even Captain Thompson's putty job can't hide the fact that fatherhood isn't agreeing with him, I'm sent back to class.

Third period has just begun. I find my English classroom and hand the teacher the note Ms. Hernandez gave me.

He reads it, raises his eyebrows and looks me up and down. "Welcome, Max Carrington," he says. "I'm Mr. Tatum." He runs his fingers through his mop of curly blond hair and absentmindedly scratches his head. Finally, he reaches his hand out. "Glad you could make it. We're discussing *Romeo and Juliet,* so you may want to have a seat."

"Thanks," I say, shaking his hand. I face the class and look for an empty chair. All eyes are glued on me as I make my way down the middle aisle and sit. But the strongest glare is hitting me from the second row, second seat: Kyle.

I take out my tablet, praying the cable man finally got the Internet working. I need something to mess with. They're all still gawking as Mr. Tatum resumes his lecture about Romeo's character in Act I. Mr. Tatum walks as he talks, and when he passes me he drops a worn paperback copy of the play on my desk.

After a few more minutes of pacing and discussing Romeo's view of the world, he starts asking questions. Lucky for me, the kids can't stare me down and answer Mr. Tatum at the same time.

I'm still getting a weird vibe from my right, so I give a quick sideways look.

My heart stops the second our eyes meet. I jerk my attention back to the front of the room, keeping my face as straight as possible. Crud. Supercrud.

What else can go wrong today?

Sometime over the weekend Gran warned me she'd be here, but it didn't sink into my thick skull. Probably because Gran also said that with my disguise, it wouldn't be a problem. I can't turn again, but I know it's Amber Meldon, the girl who was almost murdered by the mall nappers.

The girl I saved.

And why is she so interested in me? She can't recognize me. Even *I* don't recognize me. My hair is longer, and so brown it's almost black. My eyes aren't light hazel anymore, they're the darkest brown the Special Service could make them.

Miraculously, the computer lets me sign on to the school website. Good job, Comcast Man. I open the English class website on the tablet and concentrate very, very hard. There's a place to take notes, and that's where I'll start. I pick up the paperback and find the page Mr. Tatum is referencing, a scene toward the end of Act I. When the bell finally rings I start to get up, but a hand grips my forearm. I take a breath and look at her.

Amber smiles, her blond hair hanging loose over her shoulders. "Hi," she says. "I'm Amber."

"Hey," I say, standing. I wonder if it's too soon to feel relief that she hasn't recognized me. "I'm Max."

"Yeah, I heard," she says, her eyes never leaving mine. "Kids around here can be a little intimidating, so I wanted to say hi. If you need help or anything, let me know."

I scan the room. Mr. Tatum is thumbing through papers at his desk as the last of the students escape the classroom. I smile back at Amber. "Thanks. It hasn't been the best day so far."

She laughs, like she's heard all about it. "They'll get over it," she says, picking up her computer bag. She stuffs her copy of *Romeo and Juliet* in the side pocket. "There's an *Odyssey Junior* meeting after school if you're interested. It's the middle school news blog. We have our own site and send out a link to the latest stuff each week."

"Uh, thanks, but I've got lacrosse practice."

"Okay," she says. "But I won't give up on you. I lost my best writer a few weeks ago and I need to replace him. Maybe since you're a jock you can write about sports—a sort of inside view of your team or something. Or you can help me report on the school elections. They're next week."

I don't remember Amber being so, uh, pushy—she's reminding me of Laci, who happens to be her best friend.

They're on a gymnastics team together. The same Laci that Toby has a huge crush on. I like her, too.

I mean, I don't. Not in *that* way.

What I mean is, it's complicated.

Amber leans in, waiting for my answer. It's like she doesn't want this conversation to end without me saying I'll help her. Definitely like Laci. "Um, I'm not exactly a writer."

At first I think she's gonna argue, but she doesn't. Instead, her eyes suddenly sweep from my bow tie all the way down to my spiffy black shoes, and then back again to meet mine. She begins a slow walk toward the door. I'm off the hook.

I start to follow her, but then she pauses and looks briefly at Mr. Tatum. He's completely focused on the laptop now open in front of him. She faces me again. "Max," she says, slowly drawing out my name.

I wait, but she doesn't say anything. And the silence is awkward, 'cause we're both standing like statues, looking at each other from across the room.

I step closer. "Yeah?"

Amber takes a breath and then shrugs. "No big deal. It's just that I've gone to school here since fourth grade. Sydney Brown is...hard to explain. Be careful, especially if you have opinions—or think you do."

I laugh at that. "Don't worry, I don't have opinions. Not even one."

Laci's best friend gives me one more smile. "Perfect. People with no opinions make the best reporters." Then she walks into the hallway.

Yeah, perfect.

# 8

"What *are* you?"

Yup. It's been a long two hours since Amber tried to warn me, and now, sitting at this table, I understand what she meant: at Sydney Brown School, I need to think hard before I answer a question like that.

I glance from the lanky kid wearing the iridescent bow tie in a startling lime-green plaid, down to my plate of sautéed kale, blackened triggerfish, jalapeño cheese grits and Napa cabbage slaw. A man in a tall white chef's hat standing behind the sneeze guard told me I should try to get to late lunch early if I expect any Havarti macaroni and cheese, apparently a Sydney Brown School favorite. Then he sprinkled fresh parsley over my fish.

No kidding.

I am utterly confused. Not only is my stomach screaming for sausage pizza, I'm not sure the rest of me can function without it.

Reluctantly, I pick up the fork, which is heavier than a piece of Gran's family silver, and look back to the Harvard graduate-in-training, who has, unfortunately, *not* gone away and wants to know *what* I am.

This school is off-the-charts crazy. I've met at least five kids of congresspeople and senators, the grandson of a Supreme Court justice, the daughter of an admiral, the twin sons of some diplomat from Turkey, and the great-grandnephew of one of the Kennedys—and they've each asked some version of that same question.

Democrat or Republican? Christian, Jewish, Muslim or other? Where did your parents go to school? Are you a US citizen? How many moms do you have? Are you a boarder or a commuter? Who will you support for student government president, Peter or Monique? What do you think of the current immigration policy? Do you have a girlfriend? Do you *like* girls?

The Special Service has changed my hair and eye color. They've given me a new name, a new history and fake parents—even killed one of them off. They didn't tell me how to answer questions like these.

But at Sydney Brown, *what* I am seems to matter more than anything else. It would be so much easier if I could tell them I'm a spy, or an undercover bodyguard. At least I might get a few laughs—especially after this morning.

I decide to stick with what I've been saying: not much.

"Uh, I'm a lacrosse player, I guess." I roll a bite of fish around in the grits, stab my fork into the slaw and stick the combo in my mouth. Grown-up food, but the best thing is, it'll keep me busy chewing for a while.

"No," he says as he sits. He swipes his longish brown hair back with his fingers and picks up his fork. "I mean, we need to know how to register you—what side you'll be on for the elections: Stripes or Stars. It determines everything at SB. What parties you'll be invited to, who your friends will be. Where you'll go to college." His lip curls like a dog warning me off. "Lacrosse doesn't tell me anything— you won't play, anyway."

How does he know I won't play?

"So what about your parents? Are they more traditional, or do they want to save the planet from melting icebergs?"

I can't shovel another bite fast enough. I have no idea how to respond to that. Agent Brick didn't tell me. I'm beginning to think we must have skipped the most important binder.

One thing's for sure, I can't answer. Not now, at least.

I swallow and look down at my plate. Somehow, it's mostly empty.

No more stalling.

I reach my hand across the table and force my new name into the space between us. "I'm Max Carrington."

He takes my hand with a firmer-than-necessary grip and squeezes tight. "Otto Penrod the Third. My dad went to Harvard and is the Speaker of the House. And I hate to break it to you, but after the way you went after Kyle this morning, everybody knows your name. It's like you've been put on a terrorist watch list or something."

I figured Harvard had something to do with this. But the rest of his speech is a blur. His dad speaks at a house? Why do people keep telling me about their parents? And a terrorist watch list? *Me?*

Otto waves his hand, shaking his head, like it's no big deal—but his tone says otherwise. "No, I don't care. I'll let the CIA worry about your trip to Guantánamo. My job is to know the inside scoop—about *everybody*. See that kid over there?" He points to the food line. "His mom's about to be appointed attorney general." Then he gestures to a table right beside us. "And that girl? Her dad is being held hostage in Syria. Fifty-two days and counting." Otto shifts in his seat, turning back to me. "My dad runs the political world of DC. I run the one here. I'm also Peter's campaign manager, and I'm here to tell you voting Stripes will get you farther at SB, and in your career. So are you with us?"

*Career?* He sounds like a friggin' grown-up. I don't even know Peter, or the other person who's running. For a second Laci's green eyes and her big smile—the nice one—flash in my memory, back to when she wanted me to be her vice-president. Some people get so weird about elections. And college. And life.

Otto is waiting for my answer, his narrowed eyes pushing me to commit, one way or the other. But he's been running this conversation, and like on the lacrosse field, I gotta get control of the ball.

I stand and take my tray as I slide my chair back. "Let's just say I'm undecided. See you around." Then I head to the door, with a casual look to where Kyle is sitting with a group of kids. Lacrosse players?

He catches me watching and immediately looks away with a *What is* that *guy still doing here?* expression.

The Special Service made sure I was in every single one of his classes, but after my big screw-up, I'm not sure that was a good idea. The guy will do anything he can to avoid me.

Between blowing any possible friendship with Kyle and figuring out "what" I am, I need help.

I push through the cafeteria doors and pull out my SpiPhone. Quickly, I type the password, press my thumb against the screen and hit the Special Service text icon.

I select Gran's name and type as I walk.

**They want to know what I am. Like religion and if my dad is saving the planet, and other stuff. IMPORTANT. Need help!!!**

The response from Gran is immediate. And *not* helpful.

**Will discuss at dinner. Stay on task: Stay close to your friend!**

Close to my friend? Very funny.

I shoved him into a toilet stall—and we hadn't even been introduced.

Grandmothers obviously don't get what's acceptable under the bro code rules of conduct.

9

Lacrosse practice. Usually I'd be looking forward to it. Now, not so much. I'd even prefer Amber's news blog meeting to this.

I open my assigned locker and start to get changed. They have practice uniforms here. Black and gold. *Practice. Uniforms.* I hold up my new swag. Lucky for me, my SB number is 13.

Whoever managed my infiltration into Sydney Brown life did a thorough job. They got me into all Kyle's classes, and the same lunch period and now my lacrosse locker is three steps away; we're practically forced to share a bench.

The rest of the guys are mostly dressed as I sit down to put on my cleats, keeping my eyes on my laces, not Kyle's struggle with his shoulder pads. Or Agent Kang, who stands less than ten feet away, staring us down. Yep. The Special Service planted a serious surveillance wall around the guy, and I ruined it before first period was over. Now that wall is sprouting a healthy crop of creep factor.

I'm the creep.

I need a plan to turn this around.

I grab my helmet and stick and follow a group of guys out the door. Beyond the locker room door there's a fleet of golf carts parked in a small paved lot. I saw the maintenance crew and staff whipping around the pathways earlier as I looked out the windows during the day, but jeez, how many do they need?

There's a cool breeze, and my shoulders start to relax as I make my way up the hill with my new teammates. When we crest it, the view stretches far and wide. I haven't been on this campus since we played SB last year, and I'd forgotten how awesome it is. Five different playing fields span several acres—baseball, soccer, lacrosse and a couple that look generic. Then there's a full-sized track and several tennis courts. It's hard to believe this much open land lies just a couple of miles from the White House.

Behind the baseball field, and even farther away, there's a rooftop barely visible beyond a thick line of woods. That must be the dorm Agent Brick told me about—she said a lot of kids live here during the week because their parents travel so much for work.

I take it back: SB does need a fleet of golf carts. Not only that, they should let the kids who live in the dorm drive them.

A guy bumps against me as he passes with his gear, and we lock eyes. He quickly looks away, and a funny feeling tingles down my spine. Everybody else can't stop staring at me, asking questions. Not this guy.

I'm about to catch up, maybe introduce myself, when I get bumped again. It's Otto, the guy from the cafeteria.

Sorry, Mr. Harvard. Still undecided.

"What position?" he asks, a challenge in his tone.

Gramps always said some guys think they're in charge of the way life will play out, not just for themselves, but for everyone else, too. I've officially met one of them.

We're almost to the lacrosse field, and I shrug. "I hear it doesn't matter. I'm not gonna play."

Then I split away from him and find a spot for my bag, keeping tabs on Kyle in a not-so-obvious-look-at-everybody-else-instead sort of way. He's already on the field, throwing in a group of three.

There are two men on the sideline, watching another coach clock shots with a radar gun. That's cool. I hit 70 mph when we used one at Masters, but I mostly averaged about 66 or 67.

I scoop a random ball and head over to the two men. I hold out my hand to the tall one as I approach. He looks like the photo of the head coach Agent Brick showed me. "Coach, I'm Max Carrington."

He grabs my hand. "I'm Coach Pearce." He looks me up and down and grimaces. "We've got one more game and then play-offs. What's your position?"

Everybody is so happy to have me around. "Attack. Left. Sometimes middie."

He shakes his head, like his roster is full of attackmen, then nods to the other man. "Hard to say if you'll get any time on the clock until next year, but we'll keep an eye on you. For now, jump in and we'll see how you fit."

I take that as a dismissal and turn to join my new team-mates, who are in warm-up mode, some throwing, others in line for the radar gun. *Nobody* is goofing off.

The kid who bumped me earlier is at the opposite goal, by himself. He's got a few balls lined up beside him and is taking shots. I guess if I have to get to know these guys, I might as well start with him. I watch him as I jog toward the goal. He's got a wicked fast shot, and I wonder why they're not clocking him. He's got to be a starter.

When he takes his stick back again I let my ball fly, and it blows into the upper left corner of the net, maybe three inches shy of his.

He jerks and snaps his head as he realizes somebody's behind him. It's the kind of thing Toby and I do to each other all the time, sneaking up and taking a shadow shot, so it's a surprise to see the bug-out expression in his eyes.

"Sorry," I say. "Didn't mean to spook you." I mean it, but this guy looks doubtful.

He picks up another ball. "You didn't."

"I'm Cla—er, I'm Max," I say. I want to kick myself. It's really hard to get used to a different name. "I'm new."

Midshot, he freezes. He slowly turns to face me. "You just got here? Today?"

He's got an accent, but I can't place it. Northern? Southern? Venezuelan?

"Yeah."

"Weird to switch schools in May."

Something is off with this kid. He's talking to me, but at the same time his eyes are like a pinball, the way they're pinging each corner of the field.

"Yeah, my dad got brought in for some big project, so here I am." Agent Brick told me, whenever I'm answering questions, stick with basics and don't share any details if at all possible. And then take the spotlight off myself and shine it right back on them ASAP. That way I don't get stuck answering questions like the one Comcast Man shot at me this morning when he asked where I lived before.

"What about you?"

He stares at me for a few seconds. "I got here a few months ago."

He's not an SB lifer, but he's not brand-new, either.

I keep the spotlight on him. "Your dad's job, too?"

"It's only me and my mom," he says, bringing his stick back.

I watch the ball fire out of his stick. It skirts the grass line and hits the back of the goal. I scoop a ball from a few feet away and take my own shot. But I'm not thinking about the goal.

"So, what's your name?" I say.

Again he hesitates before he answers. "James."

And just as I'm sketching a mental picture to figure out if and how James might help me fit in around here, Coach Pearce blows his whistle, and the drills begin.

This team works out hard. On top of speed and agility drills with sticks in hand and balls flying, the SB guys also run serious sprints between drills. Even the goalie. And they practice things I've never heard of before, like deceleration. *Deceleration?* I must've landed on another planet.

We're half an hour into practice and I'm ready to drop. I look around at everybody else, and it's a regular day for them. They could probably go for hours like this. Even James seems okay, except for the fact that Otto keeps messing with him.

I'm watching Otto thrust his stick into James's shoulder

pads for the thousandth time when I notice something: Otto's jersey. He's number 23. I may not be great at math, but I'm awesome at remembering numbers. Number 23 is the one Percy told the Masters team about at lunch last week: the player who sends opponents to the sidelines.

No wonder James is jumpy. It all makes sense. But the kid's got more-than-solid skills. Why does he dance around Otto when he obviously has the talent to outplay him? Or at least challenge the guy?

Coach blows his whistle and calls us in. Once we're gathered around, he holds his hand up in the universal *shut your mouths* signal.

"Our final game of the season, as you know, is against Masters on Wednesday. Unfortunately, it's away, so besides their having the home advantage"—he pauses—"there will be the usual security issues to deal with." Then he waves his clipboard above his head. "That means we have two days of practice. Boys, we need to be ready. A win against Masters gives us a great advantage in the play-offs."

The good news is, from what Coach Pearce said earlier, it's not likely I'll get on the field against my own team. The bad news is, I'll be on Masters turf, sitting on the wrong bench.

A few guys start jabbering, and Coach holds his clipboard up again with a stern look. Immediate silence.

"But as you also know, we have a problem. Our face-off specialists, Jeremy and Winston, were injured in Saturday's game against St. Patrick's, and it's doubtful either of them will be ready to play this week." His eyes pass over the entire team. "That means a couple of you will have to step up. So we're going to do some one-on-one drills and select four of you to focus on face-offs tomorrow."

I've got a strange feeling that someone's watching me and look to my left. I'm wrong. It's not one person, it's two. Otto and Kyle are standing together, seriously boring into me. Just my luck: they're friends.

I don't know why they're singling me out, but the message is clear: *Don't even think about it. You aren't going to face off on* our *field.*

The hidden language of guys: it all comes down to respect. They'll treat me like Otto's treating James if I don't earn it right here. And that's when I know, even though face-offs aren't my biggest strength, and even though the last thing I want to do is go against my Masters teammates, and even though this workout has almost killed me, it's time to dig deep.

Winning that ball is my ticket to straightening out my life at Sydney Brown. It's the only way I'll be able to get Otto off my case and maybe have a second chance with Kyle. 'Cause he's sure not gonna invite me to the White House for a sleepover the way things stand now.

I stare right back at them.

# 10

Captain Thompson and I stand in the empty, odorless kitchen, the captain getting ready to call for pizza, when Gran bursts through the garage door loaded with Big Stone's bags.

Gran's eyes flit doubtfully between the captain and me as we pounce on the bags and start unloading onto the table. She shakes her head and sends a semiamused glare to Captain T. "You were calling the pizza place, weren't you? Is that your answer to dinner *every* night, Derek?"

"Liza, the last time I used a stove I had to call the fire department." Captain Thompson screws up his face and shakes his head. "I doubt you want to attract that sort of attention."

Gran clamps her lips together and disappears into the pantry so fast her heels throw out sparks.

Poor Captain Thompson; he should know by now.

A second later Gran returns holding a titanic red fire extinguisher. "In case of emergency," she says. "And there's another one in the garage. By the time I'm through, not only will you be able to boil water, you'll be able to roast a chicken, sear a steak and julienne vegetables, and this house will remain standing. Is that clear?"

Captain Thompson grunts some assurance that sounds like "when pigs fly," and then laughs as he opens the Big Stone's bag in his hands. "You just want me to be able to fill in for Carlos at the diner."

Gran sits in her chair and sets the fire extinguisher on the floor. She wags her finger at the captain. "Show some respect," she says, with an I'm-only-half-kidding smile. "Speaking of Carlos, he's rather busy with his new assignment. So yes, if you *could* cook, that's exactly where I'd send you."

"What's Carlos doing?" I ask, grabbing my own Big Stone's bag. There's a box labeled LASAGNA and another labeled CAESAR SALAD. Exactly what I want. I know the lasagna is Carlos's secret recipe.

I glance up from dishing a piece onto my plate and catch Gran shooting the captain her famous warning look.

She's gotta do better than that if she wants to keep secrets. "What's going on?"

Captain Thompson shrugs like it's no big deal and unwraps his burger. "We're helping the US Marshals transport a federal witness, that's all. It's a particularly dangerous assignment because a Mafia family is involved."

"What do the US Marshals do?" I cut a piece of lasagna and bring it to my mouth, a thick string of cheese hanging from my fork.

"It'd be easier to tell you what they don't do," Gran answers. "But in this situation, they're trying to keep a witness alive before, during and after testimony through their federal Witness Security Program. Some people call it Witness Protection. Generally they don't involve other agencies, but in this case they need a driver with a unique set of skills—and we are able to provide some help."

"Carlos?"

Captain Thompson nods. "He's one of the top tactical drivers in this country, maybe even the world."

I park food inside my cheek so I can talk, and hope Gran doesn't notice. "Who's the witness? Somebody important?"

I close my mouth and chew as Gran stares at me for a second before answering. "We don't know, Clayton. And yes, they are important, because they're important to the case. But the marshals keep their identities top secret."

"They won't even tell *you*?"

"That's right. And they shouldn't. It would put the witness and the family and friends in jeopardy." Gran lifts a forkful of steamed broccoli to her mouth. "Now let's discuss other top secret information that hopefully won't get us all killed."

Might as well get it over with. "Er, I'm sorry about what happened this morning," I say. "I knew that box probably wasn't a bomb, but what if it had been?"

Gran nods. "You screwed up splendidly, Clayton. But in your place I would likely have made the same decision."

I clear my throat. "The thing is, I think it's ruined the assignment. Forget being friends, Kyle would like me to disappear. And then there's his bestie, the great and powerful Otto Penrod the Third. I'm pretty sure *he's* gonna have me assassinated or something."

"Penrod? You mean Otto Penrod's *son*? The Speaker of the House, Otto Penrod?"

I nod. "Yeah."

Gran lets out a long breath. "You've got your hands full if he's anything like his father."

Captain Thompson leans back. "And he's friends with Kyle? That's a surprise."

"No kidding," I say. "See what you've gotten me into?"

Gran smiles. "Nothing you can't handle, dear. Now tell us, what else has happened today? Anything that stands out besides Otto?"

I think back to practice. "There's another new kid I can't figure out."

Captain Thompson's body snaps forward like a rubber band. "What *other* new kid?"

"I met him at practice. His name is James, and he arrived a few months ago. It doesn't seem like he fits in, or wants to. Sort of a loner."

Captain Thompson looks at Gran. "He didn't come up as a concern when we looked at student and staff profiles. Do you know anything about him?"

"Nothing. I'll call Frankie after dinner. By morning, we'll know all there is to know." Gran shakes her head before continuing. "I've been keeping up with this sudden flurry of Internet postings naming Sydney Brown. We're tracking IP addresses, but so far they're all dead ends. It's very unusual for a school to be named on these sites. When you add the records breach, it's doubly concerning, although my people are telling me that appears to be a simple one-time data grab."

Captain Thompson grimaces. "Have the online messages become more specific? We don't usually get reports like this unless a significant threat is in the works."

Gran leans toward the captain and shrugs. "Not more specific, but on my way here I received another alert. The increase in references to Sydney Brown is certainly getting our attention. I'm going to send Jones and Brick over to take a look around the school tonight while Kyle's detail isn't present. I want to make sure we don't miss a thing."

Captain Thompson nods his agreement, then returns his focus to me. "Anything else we should know about?"

"Well, that cable repairman asked me where I was from. He's probably the weirdest adult I met."

Captain Thompson frowns. "Clayton, you don't need to worry about him. We have folks checking out staff and adults at the school. Got it?"

"Yes, sir."

Gran gives a little harrumph. "I've found that it's not the weird people you need to worry about. It's the ones who blend in. The better they melt into their surroundings, the better they are at fooling us. It's the same on our side of the law. You stick to blending in, Clayton, and you'll do a fine job at Sydney Brown."

The captain pushes his chair back and picks up his dish. "Yes, it's crucial that you stay focused on Kyle and his whereabouts. Someone might be posing as a kid, contacting Kyle and convincing him to meet off-campus. Or someone could have convinced one of his friends to help get to him. If you overhear any conversations, or happen to see his texts, those are things we need to know about."

I follow him to the sink, shaking my head. "Yeah, right. Didn't you hear? I can't get within three yards of the guy."

The captain chuckles. "Like your grandmother said, you'll figure it out."

This job of being a regular kid and making friends with Kyle has turned from simple to complicated, and now it's starting to seem impossible. Which reminds me. "Uh, another thing. These Sydney Brown kids are off-the-charts in my business. I've never been asked so many questions in my life."

"What are you having trouble with?" says Gran.

I pause to think for a second. "There's this Stars versus Stripes thing for the school election. I'm supposed to choose, and that kid Otto is being a pain about it."

"A pain?" says the Captain.

"Yeah, as in, I won't get into Harvard if I don't join his precious Stripes party." Even the thought of it makes me cringe. "Me. Harvard. That's a good one."

Gran's lips are thin, and she sounds disappointed when she speaks. "Aren't school elections still about longer lunch periods and more school dances? When I was your age there weren't any 'parties,' and anybody could run with enough signatures."

"Don't look at me," I say. "Elections aren't like this at Masters."

Captain Thompson shrugs. "I'm not surprised. SB parents are all involved in politics somehow. But I think the answer to your problem is pretty simple: whatever Kyle is, that's what you are."

It sort of feels good, talking school stuff through like a real family, with Gran and Captain Thompson in the kitchen—the way I used to with my parents.

"Okay, I'm going to go to school tomorrow and find out as much as I can about Kyle. By lunch I'll know what side I need to be on, Stripes or Stars."

Gran narrows her eyes. "You sound confident, Clayton. How are you going to do that?"

"Don't worry," I say. "I know exactly who to ask."

## tuesday, May 8, 6:15 a.m.

# 11

Tuesday starts out weird. There's an identity specialist sitting on my bed when I get out of the shower. He wants to check my nose implant and see if I need any help with my Max Carrington look, and I'm not allowed to leave my bedroom without his approval.

Every morning I'm gonna go through this?

Gran's Breakfast Special—a toasted bagel with peanut butter, a glass of orange juice and a banana—makes the surprise agent a bit more forgivable.

When we reach school in the limo, the Special Service chauffeur opens the rear door and nods to me as I get out. Like yesterday, he hands me my stuff with an under-the-breath "Good luck, kid." Except today we're early, and there are a lot more witnesses. These kids must really like school to get here before first bell.

I walk through the Sydney Brown entrance with a high-priority item on my to-do list: track down Amber and get her to tell me everything she knows about Kyle. I know she knows him. Her stepdad and the president used to be friends. Plus she's on the news blog staff. And she's a girl.

Add those things together and Amber Meldon is my Wikipedia. The question is, will she spill? And the answer is, she will, if I figure out a way to tell her I'm not Max Carrington.

But should I do that?

When I approach my locker, it's cracked open—and empty. I left it empty, but I also made sure it was closed. Somebody has been in it. I glance sideways as I slide my backpack inside.

Agent Kang and some other suits are standing where the hall intersects with another wing, a few feet from where Kyle is unloading stuff into his locker. I don't know how Kang can watch me while he stares straight ahead, but that's what he's doing.

I close my locker and pull hard to be sure it's actually shut—even though *that* obviously doesn't matter around here. As I turn, my shoe hits something and I bend down to the carpet. It's a pen, and not just any pen. It's a black pen with President Hampton's signature and seal, both in gold. I pick it up and send Agent Kang an accusing look. Guess I know who messed with my locker.

I stick my new souvenir in my pocket and look down the hall, toward Advanced World History. Not ready for that yet. Suddenly my newfangled nose gets a strong whiff of something familiar. I remember hearing about a snack area at the end of the east hallway; it's where kids hang out before school.

I pretend to adjust the strap of my computer bag as I take another look around. Kang and his posse obviously have Kyle under control at the moment, so why not follow the scent of roasting coffee beans? I'm supposed to get to know this place. Maybe I'll even find Amber along the way.

I walk past the presidential junior entourage, feeling the heat of Kang's glare-stare on my back as I right-angle it and head down the east hallway. I remember Captain Thompson's reminder, so I put myself on high alert for stuff like exit doors, out-of-place backpacks, boxes that don't contain science projects, and undercover assassins—while also keeping an eye out for Amber.

There are school cameras every thirty feet or so, on opposite sides of the hallway. Most of them are anchored to the ceiling, but I also notice one attached to the rim of a wall clock, and another on the tip of a watercooler jug. I wonder if those are Agent Kang's. None of them are Special Service—not yet, anyway—but I also know Gran can tap into any of them with her spy satellites.

The kids at their lockers seem pretty normal as they get ready for school to start. I move toward the end of the hall, and the voices from a crowd are getting louder even though I don't see anything.

Just then, a hand swoops in from the right, linking with my arm. I gasp, shutting down the reflex to jump three feet and run, and look into the light brown eyes I've been searching the halls for.

"I wouldn't think you'd be the type to startle so easily," says Amber.

Why the heck would she say that? She doesn't know me—or, at least, she thinks she doesn't.

I shrug and give her my best laugh-it-off response. "I haven't had any caffeine yet."

"Caffeine *makes* you jumpy, Max," she says as we round the corner together.

The scene in front of us is like nothing I've ever seen at a school. There's a long counter in front of a coffee bar with a full-on espresso machine, complete with the aroma of strong coffee and the whooshing noise of steaming hot milk. Farther down there are two side-by-side blenders munching ice for frozen drinks. And just like in a real coffee shop, there's a display of donuts and bagels and breakfast sandwiches.

Amber leads me through a crowd of kids clamoring around two narrow tables set across from each other. The tables are each decorated according to their party: one with stars, the other with stripes. Obviously this is the hangout for the student government campaigns.

Amber nudges me and gives me an *Earth to Clayton*—or *Max*—look. "So what do you want?"

"A mocha, I guess," I say, noticing the guy in front of us using his student ID card to pay. I start to pull mine out.

"No," says Amber, whipping hers from a yellow leather pouch hanging against her hip. "I got this. Sort of a 'Welcome to Sydney Brown.'" She steps ahead as the line moves, and turns back to me. "So, how was your first day?"

I laugh. "Exactly like you warned me. Apparently, I gotta figure out who I am, by yesterday."

Amber squeezes my arm. "That's the real problem, Max. They don't want to know *who* you are. They want to know *what* you are."

Before I can respond, she orders our drinks and swipes her student ID. Less than two minutes later she's leading me to an empty set of chairs, a little removed from all the chaos of the battling campaign tables. I sit with my back to the wall so I can watch the room as we talk, something I remember my grandfather always did, even though I didn't realize why at the time.

I recognize the two kids running against each other for president from all the posters hanging on the school walls: Peter and Monique. They're both surrounded by their minions, who are laughing and chattering as if there's nowhere they'd rather be. All but Otto Penrod *the Third*, that is. He's got his arms folded and is leaning over Peter's shoulder, talking with an annoyed expression squeezed firmly between his eyebrows.

Other kids are scattered around, some finishing homework, or eating breakfast, or doing the antisocial thing with earbuds plugged into their phones. There are even some adults, probably teachers, clutching their own paper cups. I look at the dwindling line at the coffee bar and notice the cable guy I saw yesterday. I know Gran said they double-checked everybody, but it's strange how he keeps popping up. If SB is still having Internet problems, Ms. Hernandez must be pretty mad by now.

Amber clears her throat to get my attention. When I meet her gaze she leans forward in her chair and takes a sip of her chai latte. "I need to talk to you."

Oh, yeah. I need to talk to *her.*

I taste my mocha. It's really good. Amber is scooting even closer, and next thing I know her whole face is less than three inches away from my fake nose.

Sheesh. Talk about intense. Why do kids like Amber and Laci always work so hard to convince you to do stuff you don't want to do, like run for student government vice-president or write for the school news blog?

"What's up?" Her lips barely move when she whispers, "Why are you here, Clayton—dressed like that?"

I'm still. Only my eyes move, first to the left and then to the right, scanning the scene around us as I process what she just said. Gran is gonna freak.

"Uh. What do you mean?"

She hesitates before whispering, "I heard your voice; it was familiar. And then—"

She reaches for my hand and rubs my wrist without taking her eyes from mine. I look down. She flips her own hand over, and then I see: her wrist, and our identical scars, from the ropes that tied us less than a month ago. Amber's scar is deeper on the outside, but we'll both be carrying the memory of her kidnapping around for a long while.

I'm not sure what to do, so I start by stating the obvious. "You can't tell anybody."

She waves me off as she relaxes into her chair. "Of course I know that, *Max*." She says my fake name with emphasis, and then lowers her voice again. "But is something big going on? Something bad?"

I give up. I was going to tell her anyway. Okay, I was *considering* it. "Sort of." I take a breath before explaining. "It's about Kyle. Actually, I could use your help."

"Oh, no. Is he in danger?"

"I'm trying to figure that out," I say. "You know him—has he been acting strange lately?"

Amber halfway stands, then sits and crosses her legs. "Well," she says, avoiding my eyes, "you're right. We've known each other a long time, and I even thought we were sort of best friends. But then he suddenly started hanging out with Otto, and now he barely knows my name." She tilts her head as she gets to the point. "So, yeah, Kyle's been acting strange lately."

Oh. Wow. This is exactly the sort of information Gran needs. I've got to find out more.

"Have you asked him what's up?"

Amber only shrugs and rolls her eyes. "He says Otto is better than I think and I should give him a chance."

The bell rings, and my heart starts beating against my rib cage. This conversation barely got started. I need answers *now*.

"Can we talk sometime this morning? This is pretty important," I say, watching the students packing up, in a rush to make it to their first classes.

"No problem," she says, standing. "But the lowdown on Kyle is going to cost. You're going to have to help *me* help *you*." There's a satisfied gleam in her eyes as she grins and holds out her hand for a shake. "Max Carrington, welcome to *Odyssey Junior*."

I let out a small groan and shake her hand. I should have known. In the end, girls always find a way to get exactly what they want.

# 12

I'm heading to World History when I get knocked from behind. It's Otto Penrod *the Third*.

"Looks like you lucked out," he says.

I can't wait to hear. Did I win free mochas for a year? A million dollars? Oh, I know: he's going to teleport me back to Masters so I can play lacrosse on a team that wants me.

He squints his right eye, and the corner of his mouth twitches in a smirk. This guy's trying to mess with me like we're longtime rivals. Gramps wouldn't play—not without a ball, at least. I'm not gonna, either. I keep walking.

I feel him like a shadow, half a step behind but with me, pace for pace. I try to keep cool and remember I'm not here to make friends. I'm here for Kyle.

"Yeah," Otto says. It's practically a sneer. "Mr. Undecided made it through the face-off drills."

I made the cut? An excited tingle starts to run through me—but Otto is killing the mood. Dang it. No victory dance.

I stop and face him. "Thanks for letting me know."

He puffs himself up, like he thinks he's the Hulk or something. "Yeah, I told you I get all the news. But I have to say, I've been digging, and there's nothing out there about you—or your parents. I'm not sure you're cut out to be with the Stripes. What's the real story?"

This guy is unbelievable. "Story? No story. I only want to play some lacrosse and finish the school year. That's it."

"Yeah, right. Everybody has a story. And the harder I have to look, the better it usually turns out to be." Otto snickers. "Just ask Peter in a few hours."

My fingers clench into fists. Every gut instinct says to ignore this guy, but holy mother of me when I'm mad, I wish I could tell him to shut up. I hear Gramps in my head: *Do the smart thing.*

So I clamp down on my mouth and exit Otto's esteemed presence, counting the whole thirty-five seconds it takes me to get to World History.

I stand in the front of the classroom, still counting. If I'm not careful, Otto will distract me from the real reason I'm here, and that's no good.

I move down the aisle and sit next to the kid who doesn't like me. Yet.

"So," I say under my breath, but loud enough for Kyle to hear, "did I miss anything yesterday? The Secret Service needed to consult me on their rescue response time drill."

I look over just as he coughs an unwilling laugh. He turns to me and shakes his head, biting down a grin. "Funny," he says.

"Yeah, well, I'm seriously sorry. I guess my patriotic duty gene went into overdrive." I stick out my hand. "Listen, man, I will never again tackle you in a bathroom or anywhere else without express permission from you or your father. I swear."

Kyle eyes me for a second and then shrugs and accepts my hand. "I guess somebody's got to give my bodyguards something to do."

And then he tells me what I missed in Advanced World History yesterday.

★

The rest of the class goes okay. It's doubtful Kyle and I will ever be best buds, but at least now we have an understanding that doesn't include a death stare every time I break his ten-foot-radius barrier. And even if I said it like a joke, I told him exactly what my job is and how I'm gonna operate.

The morning goes by at reverse warp speed, but somehow I live through the 2,880 seconds of second-period Algebra I. No surprise that the First Kid is a heckuva lot brainier than me when it comes to math. I'm on my way to English when an old lady with a bucket bends to the floor in front of me. I try to sidestep her, but she reaches out and touches my arm.

"Young man, do you think you could help me with this?" she says, standing. She's still a little hunched over as she hands me the bucket.

There's a janitor's closet a few feet away, and she opens the door, gesturing for me to follow. "If you could help me fill that, I would be eternally grateful."

I'm starting to stammer an excuse about being late for class when, in a hardly visible movement, she grabs my wrist and hauls me inside, whipping the door shut behind us. She snatches the bucket, sets it in the deep janitor's sink, turns the water on full blast and then stands absolutely straight as a rod and lifts a single eyebrow. "Clayton

Stone, I thought I taught you, never hesitate to help those in need."

I look closer at the steely blue eyes staring back at me. "Gran?"

She gives me a smug, satisfied smile, showing off hard-to-tell-they're-fake yellowed teeth. "Who else?"

I shake my head. "What is it with you and closets?"

Gran chuckles and pulls a phone from somewhere inside the folds of her housekeeper getup. "I find them very useful," she says as she taps the screen. "But we don't have much time. I need to brief you on several things, so listen carefully."

"Is something going on?"

"Clayton, this is not the time for silly questions. Something is *always* going on. This time, I'm advising you about the situation."

I stand a little taller, remembering something Gramps always said. "Oh, yeah. It's called the need-to-know basis."

"What you *need to know* is how to *listen*," she retorts. "And if you were paying attention at dinner yesterday, you'll remember that Jones and Brick were sent to conduct a thorough search of the school's premises in the middle of the night."

"Did they find anything?"

Gran nods. "While they were on the path between the dorms and the school, they spotted a man lurking in the woods. They lost him but took a careful look around the dorms. Unfortunately, they could not get inside without identifying themselves, but they did find a camera, distinct from the Sydney Brown security system. It was attached to a light post and aimed at the dorm entrance."

"Wow. Really?"

"Yes. They screened other lights and found another camera aimed at the school's main entrance. We've left both in place and will monitor them, but this is alarming, especially considering that in the past twelve hours we've found two more coded posts. We're busy trying to decipher the messages, but one thing we do know is that both Sydney Brown and lacrosse were mentioned."

In the last twelve hours? That's strange. The only thing different about the lacrosse team at SB in the last twelve hours is *me*.

Gran pulls a pink slip out of her pocket and hands it to me. "Your hall pass," she says, with a look to the now-overflowing bucket. "Oh, and I almost forgot. A preliminary search reveals no background information beyond the surface level on James Scott, the new student you mentioned. Probably nothing to be concerned about; I only want you to be aware that he's currently a watch."

"What does that mean?"

"It means you pay attention and we keep probing. Hopefully we'll discover that one of his parents has top secret clearance, and that will eliminate him as a risk. You should press him for information about his family."

"Okay. But Gran, I really think you should check out that cable guy again. I mean, you got in here, right?"

She turns off the faucet, empties most of the water out of the bucket and lifts it from the sink. "Clayton, it does my heart proud that you've become so suspicious. I'll check him out personally." Then she hands me the bucket. "Now, carry this for me to the girls' bathroom. Then get to class."

I take the bucket and follow her out of the closet, into the hall, and we walk to the bathroom in silence.

"Thank you, young man," she says with a smile as I hand her the bucket. "I hope you have a very nice day."

I take a few steps and then turn back. I forgot to tell her that Amber ID'd me, but she's already disappeared into the girls' room. Guess it'll have to wait—if it's even that important.

I keep walking and examine my forged hall pass, ready for Mr. Tatum. I'm about to open the classroom door when a voice from behind surprises me. "Ready for some fun?"

It seems like every time I think of her, she appears. "You mean *Romeo and Juliet*?" I say as Amber and I enter the English classroom together.

"Nah," she says. "We're doing our own thing. If you're on *Odyssey* you get a get-out-of-jail-free card one day a week to work on news stuff."

Holy mother of the answer to my prayers. I could kiss her! Or not.

The other kids are still getting settled, but Amber yanks me across the front of the room so we're face-to-face with Mr. Tatum. Then she raises her voice. "I recruited Max for *Odyssey*. We're going to cowrite this week's articles about the election."

I hold up the hall pass Gran gave me, but Mr. Tatum ignores it. He looks from Amber to me. "I thought Mr. Hampton was your partner in crime," he says, looking past us to where Kyle is sitting. "Do you need me to talk to him?"

She answers immediately. "No," she says, quickly adding, "he's too busy for *Odyssey* these days."

"Ah," says Mr. Tatum. He grabs two of his own hall passes, signs them and hands them over. "Remember the deadline. The election's next week, so I want your pieces by Friday morning—that way the next issue can include whatever happens at the debate. We want to post your articles before school on Monday. That gives us a few days for editing." He glances back and forth between Amber and me. "You're both available?"

Amber's already dragging me toward the door. She throws an "Of course we are!" over her shoulder as we make our exit, but all I'm thinking is, this is sounding like a real job. *Another* real job.

"So, we've got forty-eight minutes," she says, still holding my arm as we turn the corner and walk down the hall. "Monique Bowling is waiting for us at the coffee bar. Then we need to track down Peter. I've texted him, but he hasn't responded." Amber's eyes flit to the ceiling. "Will you at least act like you're interested? We have a lot to do."

"We?"

"Yeah, *we*," she says. "Don't you get it? We're officially partners."

Fabulous news. I'll alert the media.

Oh, wait. I *am* the media.

# 13

Amber turns on the afterburners, as if we're late to meet the Pope. Except for a couple of suits on patrol, the halls are empty—until Comcast Man rushes past us like he's got somewhere to be, too.

I'm really glad Gran is checking him out. I don't care what anybody says, something is up with this guy.

We reach the end of the hall and turn another corner, and as we do, James comes running around it, almost knocking Amber over. He's breathing hard and his eyes are wide as he pivots backward, and I swear I see a 4.3 aftershock ripple down his body. His face flushes like he's just had the crud scared out of him and he's embarrassed about it.

"S-sorry, uh, Amber," he stammers. Then he starts forward again, and as he moves past there's a spark of recognition as he catches my eye. "Max, right? I'm crazy late—forgot my book and had to go back to the dorm. See ya."

Amber sighs and shakes her head as James disappears down the hallway. "Poor James."

"What do you mean?"

"Well, he's been here a couple of months now, and he still seems so nervous. I tried to recruit him for *Odyssey*, and he said he had too much going on." She raises her eyebrows meaningfully. "But I know for a fact that until he joined the lacrosse team he basically hid out in his dorm room like a hermit."

"I guess it's a good thing you had something to blackmail me with, or you'd be out of luck since nobody else wants to help you."

"Very funny. This is *not* blackmail; you and I are exchanging services."

"If you say so."

We keep walking, and then she grabs my arm, her face lighting up with that *I've got an idea* glow. "Hey! You play lacrosse. Maybe you can help James loosen up."

"How many jobs are you going to give me? You do know I'm here for a reason, right?"

"Come on. He needs a friend," she says.

I give up. "Okay, I'll see what I can do."

We arrive at our final destination, and I'm surprised to find a bunch of kids hanging all over the coffee bar. If I ever get back to Masters, and if I'm ever crazy enough to run for student government, building a place like this will be item number one on *my* campaign platform: somewhere to go during free periods.

"C'mon," says Amber, ushering me toward a cluster of chairs a few feet beyond one of the campaign tables. A girl with light brown skin and dark hair pulled back into smooth tiny braids stands to greet us as we approach. She reaches out with her hand and a big smile. I remind myself, Monique's got a job to do, too. She needs votes.

After I'm introduced we all sit.

Amber pulls out her phone and hits the screen a couple of times before laying it on the small table between us. "You don't mind if I record this, do you?" she says to Monique.

Monique glances briefly at the phone. "I guess that's okay."

She reaches down to a sky-blue leather tote bag, whips out a folder and then hands us a flyer outlining her campaign platform.

"As you can see, there's a lot to do at Sydney Brown," she says, gesturing to the first point on the bulleted list. "For me, one of the most important issues has to do with the girls' sports programs. We all know that most of the athletic booster money goes to improving the boys' teams, while the girls' teams are only maintained as is...."

Amber nods. "I see," she says, pointing to the third bullet point. "What about this one?"

Monique groans. "Oh, yes. The cafeteria. *That* drives me crazy. I'm not saying burgers and fries every day, but right now we get salmon once a week. We're not guests at the White House. What's next? Linen tablecloths?"

That does it: I'm voting for Monique.

After Monique's made it to the end of her list, Amber grabs her phone and stands. "I think that's all for now. I'll text you if I think of anything else, probably after I speak with Peter."

At the mention of Peter's name, Monique frowns. Amber immediately sits back down. "Is there anything else going on?"

"Not about Peter. He's nice." Monique briefly lowers her eyes and gives a small shake of her head. "It's Otto. I don't know how, but he's stealing votes from the Stars."

Sounds like regular politics to me; even if Otto is pushy, kids don't have to listen to him. Besides, voters change their minds all the time.

"Stealing? What do you mean?"

Monique looks away. "Never mind. I shouldn't have said anything."

Amber waits a few seconds before she responds. "Well, if you feel like there's something you *should* say, text me, okay?" Then she stands and touches Monique's shoulder. "I'm sorry."

Monique stares up at her. "I'm hoping Thursday's debate will change things."

Amber smiles. "Good luck. We'll get back to you if we need anything else."

I say good-bye and follow Amber into the hallway. She looks at her phone as she walks. "Okay," she says, "Peter says he'll meet us outside the study lab." She leads me up a flight of stairs to a floor I've never seen before.

Amber points a few yards away to a set of chairs. "Let's wait there."

At the click-clack of the study lab door I look to see Peter coming our way, his arm already stretched out for a shake. When he grips my hand, he looks directly into my eyes. "Peter Gallagher," he says, his whole freckled face crinkling with what might actually be a genuine smile. "Great to meet you."

"Hey," I say. "I'm Max Carrington."

Peter nods and laughs good-naturedly. "Yeah, I've heard a lot about you after yesterday. And you play lacrosse. I sort of wish I did."

"Never too late to start," I say, already liking the guy.

"Peter," says Amber, "we recorded our interview with Monique. Is it okay if we do the same with you?"

"Sure, no problem."

Amber taps her phone and sets it on the table between us, and I clear my throat. This time I'm going to ask some questions. "So, what made you decide to run for student government president?"

Peter leans back in his chair and shrugs. "My dad's a senator, so maybe the political thing runs in the family?"

"Anything else?"

"Well, it's hard to say no to Otto. He kind of runs the Stripes, and he's pretty convincing."

Amber briefly looks away. "*Convincing* is a nice way to say it. He somehow talked Kyle into leaving the Stars and joining him on the Stripes campaign."

*Good to know.* Sorry, Monique, it looks like I won't be joining the Stars anytime soon.

"It's not only Kyle," Peter laughs. "Otto is really good at convincing *everybody* to vote Stripes."

If Kyle is nice like Amber says, why would he change everything about himself to be tight with a guy like Otto? I'm confused in a big way. "Are you glad you're running?"

Peter points to Amber's cell phone. "Off the record?"

Amber reaches over the table and pokes the screen. "Sure."

Peter runs his hand through his hair and lets out a reluctant groan. "Everything *was* good. But last week I brought up what I thought were cool ideas. Stuff like starting a compost program to help with food waste, and maybe even a garden run by the students. Otto got all mad and told me to stick to the platform he and Kyle approved."

Amber's finger twitches. She probably wants to hit Record again, but she's restraining herself. "What did you do?"

Peter laughs. "I got him even madder by bringing up the composting idea in science class. Mr. Bryan thought it was awesome, and so did some of the kids."

"But it *is* an awesome idea," I say.

Amber pats me on the shoulder. "Not if Otto didn't come up with it. Plus, it's the sort of thing the Stars usually want to do. They're the ones who got the cafeteria to start using real plates and silverware, so there wouldn't be as much plastic and Styrofoam. Otto likes to stick with stuff his dad would approve."

Peter nods. "Exactly. But I figured it's my campaign, too. I should be able to push stuff I think is important. He doesn't see it that way."

"What about Kyle?" I ask. "What does he think?"

"Good question. Maybe you should ask him."

I feel his presence before I hear his voice. "Ask who what?" says Otto, hovering over us. He's glaring at Peter, who's staring back with his mouth hanging open.

Otto is swaying from the waist up, like a cobra ready to strike. "What do you think you're doing, talking to them without me here?" His head snaps toward Amber and me. "Interview over. And don't even think about—"

The bell rings before he can finish, and I reach for Amber, who's grabbed her phone. "Thanks, Peter," says

Amber. Then we stand together and move out of the line of fire. "We'll be in touch if we need anything else."

I crank my head and meet Otto's death stare as Amber tugs at my sleeve and urges me toward the stairwell. We push through the exit door together, and all I can think is, Otto seems like the last person Kyle Hampton needs as a friend.

# 14

I'm trying to forget the look on Otto's face as I enter art class, and that's hard to do. Otto not only thinks he's King of the Stripes, but he's got this weird power over everything and everyone at Sydney Brown, too, including the First Son.

He's pulled Kyle away from his friendship with Amber and convinced him to switch from the Stars to the Stripes. I think Otto is even the reason why Kyle has less to say around the family dinner table.

There's one more class before lunch, and my stomach is already sending me warning signals. Either I'm starving, or this assignment is getting to me. Either way, there's a good chance I'm gonna hurl if the SB cafeteria is serving squid salad or something equally appetizing.

I'm in a daze as I get my rolled-up art paper from yesterday and grab a spot at one of the massive tables. My brain must be working without my input, because somehow I'm sitting between Kyle and James.

With every passing minute I spend at this school, I think there's no way skittish James can be a threat to Kyle.

But Gran said he's a watch, and until he's ruled out as a threat 100 percent, my job is to protect Kyle—and today that includes finding out more about the mysterious James.

I snag a colored pencil from the tray we're sharing and start to work on the assignment. We have the week to create a story without words. It can be one scene or many, like a comic strip, but it has to be finished by Friday. So far I've drawn the outlines for three boxes. That's it: three empty squares.

I glance at Kyle, who's leaning on his elbow, using the entire piece of art paper for one big picture. He's a lot further along than I am.

I look back at my own blank boxes and wonder if I can stick-figure my way through this assignment. I force the tip of my pencil to the paper, and as I do, an image comes to me.

I don't have any other ideas, so I carefully begin to shape the eyes. After a few minutes, I'm darkening the lashes and moving on to the hair: long, with tiny wisps floating in the breeze.

"Who is she?" asks James.

I pull up my pencil, startled. I don't want to answer. "Nobody." I look at his paper, which is divided into six boxes. He's working on the third. The whole thing looks like it came out of a comic book. No kidding.

I nudge Kyle and gesture toward James.

Kyle leans over me to get a better look. He gasps, clearly as impressed as I am. "Where'd you learn to draw like that?"

James shrugs. "I took a class to learn about comics and

graphic art back in, er, at home, and since moving here I've had a lot of time to practice."

Kyle nods his appreciation. "It's good," he says as he starts coloring something in with his pencil.

"Yeah, it's really good," I say. I need to get James talking. "Comics? Like an art class? Where'd you take it?"

He stares back at me for a second before finally answering. "I don't remember."

Then he hunches over the corner of his paper and sketches letters on the license plate of an old-model sedan. The car is teetering at the end of a wooden dock, about to fall into the water, and there's an overweight guy slumped against the steering wheel. A bunch of crates full of dead fish are stacked up and down the dock, and a building stands across the street, with a shadowy figure looking on from the second-story window.

Mr. Walsh, the art teacher, drifts from student to student, praising and making suggestions as he goes. I'm definitely getting an F this period. Maybe a D-minus; my boxes are pretty good.

I start drawing again. This time it's two lacrosse players, staring at each other across the midline. Okay, they sort of look like lacrosse players. Except, my art is not what's important. Gran needs me to find out about James, only every time I try to start a conversation he either ignores me or gives a one-word answer.

I'm putting a number on the sleeve of one of my player's jerseys when I get an idea. James played on a lacrosse team before this. If I can figure out the team, that could give the Special Service something to work with. I clear my throat and have turned to James when Mr. Walsh comes up behind us.

"Pretty girl."

For a sec I'm confused, but then I feel a burn rush up my neck. "Uh, thanks."

He points to the lacrosse players and taps the midline between them. "Are they at odds?"

I look at the numbers on the jerseys—definitely didn't mean to use Toby's number. I twist in my seat and look at Mr. Walsh, not sure what to say. I turn back and put down my pencil as I stare at the girl with long dark hair. Dang it.

Before I can sputter some sort of nonstupid answer, Mr. Walsh notices what James is doing and is immediately distracted.

"May I?" he says to James.

Without another word, he carefully picks up James's paper by the top corners and proceeds to the middle of the classroom, where he clips it to an easel so the entire class can see it.

He claps twice to get our attention, then rubs his hands together as he looks more closely at the scenes James has drawn. "Look at the use of light here, ladies and gentle-men. Astounding in a black-and-white pencil drawing. Notice the way the setting sun shimmers over the rooftop and reflects off the car and the water as the car dangles precariously. Even the lifeless fish look alive. And is the man dead? Or passed out? Bravo, Mr. Scott. Well done! I wonder..."

As Mr. Walsh goes on, I hear a buzzing sound. Kyle brings his phone out of his pocket and reads a text. He scoots back and walks out of the classroom, not a word to Mr. Walsh.

I look at the clock. The bell's going to ring any second. It's lunch period. Should I follow him?

Before I can decide, the closet door opens wide and Comcast Man appears. As usual, his cap is slanted forward, but for the first time I clearly see his licorice-black eyes. The way they're bulging as he stares at me, at James and at Kyle's empty spot paralyzes me for a long second— then he hightails it out the door, right after Kyle.

Holy mother of undercover. A warning wave of panic ripples across my shoulders and down my arms.

I knew it! Comcast Man is not a cable repairman, he's a problem, and he's after Kyle.

Bell or not, I need to go. Now.

TUESDAY, MAY 8, 11:49 a.m.

# 15

I don't stop to put my so-called artwork away, so when the bell does ring I'm already out the door. I text Gran as I jog toward Kyle's locker—a quick *"COMCAST MAN???!!!"*—and assure myself that Kyle's security detail will be with him. They would have been somewhere outside art class, waiting.

Until this moment, it was hard to believe that there really might be a serious bad-guy-with-a-gun threat to Kyle on the inside of this school. But after the spooky way Comcast Man looked over at Kyle's empty seat and then booked out the door, my mind is officially convinced.

My phone thumps against my palm. It's Gran texting me back.

**I checked. The man working for Comcast was approved last week. He's clean. STAY with your friend.**

I slow my pace and start to turn the corner, and smash straight into my favorite person, Otto Penrod *the Third*. His jaw is set and his face is flushed and he's shaking his head in disbelief. He looks me up and down, then rolls his eyes and pushes past like I don't matter.

I'm about to take the corner again when Kyle comes whipping around it, obviously chasing after Otto. I take two steps back and press against a locker bay, 'cause I know who's coming next. Sure enough, Kang and two of his henchmen zip right after Kyle.

Down the hall they go, Kyle's security detail, Kyle and Otto. No weapons and no alarm means it's probably nothing. But where is Comcast Man?

It's a long stretch of hallway, and I follow the up-and-down motion of Kang's black suit as he tromps along. I don't run—I walk fast. I'm guessing we're headed to the cafeteria, when I start to close in and notice that the guards have stopped, yards short of where Kyle and Otto are nose to nose, in some sort of standoff.

And then I see Comcast Man, farther down, outside the cafeteria. He opens a door and waits, letting kids walk in and out, but the whole time he's staring at Otto and Kyle. Finally, he lets the door go and disappears into the cafeteria.

Kang and his men home in on me as I approach, but I act like I'm going to pass them on the way to lunch. When I'm close enough to hear, Kyle's words are slow and tight. "So you're saying it's all a huge coincidence and you don't know anything about it?"

Forget his eyes, Otto rolls his whole head, like this is the most ridiculous argument he's had in his entire life. "How many &$*@! times do I have to tell you? I don't! You shouldn't even be worrying about it; that's my job. Besides, Peter will be fine."

They both freeze when they see me, and for a second I hesitate. Should I stop?

Apparently Otto votes no, 'cause he snorts and swats his hand at me like I'm nothing but a nuisance. Then he pokes his finger at Kyle. "Just wait and see what happens, okay?" And without waiting for a response, he stomps off toward the cafeteria.

Kyle stands rigid and stuck in place as he watches Otto stalk away. "I am so sick of elections." Then he flashes an irritated look at his security detail, three suits all within yards of him, and adds under his breath, "These babysitters are getting pretty old, too."

With that Kyle takes off in the opposite direction from Otto and the cafeteria, his suits falling in behind him as though nothing happened, and as if he never even saw me.

Gran says to stay with "my friend," but as long as he's not with Otto or James and he's got his detail with him, I think Kyle's good. Plus, she didn't see the menacing look on Comcast Man's face when his eyes zoomed in on our art table a few minutes ago. It's time to do a little investigative research, 'cause that's the only way I'm gonna get to the bottom of what he's actually doing here—besides messing with the Internet. Gran needs proof before she'll listen, and this might be my only chance.

By the time I get to the cafeteria, there's no line for food. So I grab the daily special: ham, Fontina cheese, sliced apple and fig preserves on a French roll. Leave it to the SB cafeteria to layer fruit in the middle of what could have been a great sandwich.

I scan the tables for Comcast Man. It doesn't take long to find him at the very back of the cafeteria, near the outside exit. He's eating his own sandwich, but he's keeping a close watch on the entry doors. If he's waiting for Kyle, he's out of luck, but I need to find a spot for my own stakeout. I search the other tables.

Bingo. Amber's crouched in a corner on the opposite side of the large room, glued to her laptop.

When my tray hits the table, Amber looks up, a shocked expression on her face. "Do you know what's happened?"

I nod as I sit across from her. "Yep. Kyle and Otto are in a fight."

"Really?" she says, suddenly smiling.

"Yeah," I answer. "Definite trouble in paradise. But what are you talking about?"

Her smile vanishes and she spins her computer so I can see the screen. I sneak a glance over at Comcast Man, and then down at Amber's computer.

It's a page on CNN.com. I pull it closer and read the block letters: RUMORS SWIRL: DID SENATOR GALLAGHER BUY VOTES?

I take a bite of my sandwich and start to read the article. It's pretty good, actually. The sandwich, not the article. The article is terrible.

I swallow and look up at Amber. "Senator Gallagher? This is Peter's dad?"

Amber nods. "Yeah. But it's hard to believe. Peter's dad doesn't operate this way. If we were talking about Otto's dad, then yeah, but Peter's? No way."

I push the computer back to Amber. This is a world I don't want to be part of, ever. Not when I grow up, and not as a middle schooler.

Amber closes her laptop and leans over it. She lowers her voice. "I hope Peter doesn't drop out of the election because of all this."

I stare back at Amber and then down at her closed

laptop. There's something about the article that sounds familiar. "Amber, remember what Monique said about Otto this morning?"

She scrunches her eyebrows together. "You mean about him stealing Stars voters?"

"Yeah," I say. "Don't you think it's weird that it's the same sort of thing coming out about Peter's dad?"

"Now that you say it out loud, I do." She stares at me. "Why?"

"And this morning Otto said something to me about Peter, like he knew he was gonna get bad news today."

"He told you that?"

I nod. "Yep. He was trying to threaten me, saying he knows everything about everybody. He said 'Everybody has a story,' and to ask Peter later, or something like that."

Amber slowly shakes her head. "I don't like where this is going. It's impossible. You think Otto's dad is behind that story?" Then she jerks upright, her eyes wide. "Could Otto be copying his dad?"

The questions that have been somersaulting around my brain come together and launch right out my mouth. "It is possible. What if Otto knew about what his dad was doing? It makes sense. Especially when you put it together with what Monique said. What I don't understand is *how* Otto could 'steal' Stars kids and get them to vote Stripes."

Amber raises her eyebrows. "For somebody who doesn't want to be a reporter, you're asking very interesting questions. And you're making me worried. We need to figure out what Otto's up to."

I look around the cafeteria as I think. Something is not adding up.

I turn back to Amber, who's holding up both hands—empty. She hasn't come up with anything, either. "I'm going to start asking around, and then we'll decide what to do," she says.

Again with the *we*. I shake my head at her. "Amber, I told you. I'm here for Kyle, nothing else. I can't get mixed up in this election; it's too distracting."

Distracting. Oh, shoot. With all this talk about Otto, I forgot about Comcast Man. I crank my head to where he was sitting.

Dang it. He's gone.

# 16

"What is it, Max? What's wrong?"

I close my mouth and turn to Amber as I stand. Should I tell her?

No.

"Nothing. I gotta go. But start with Monique. I'll bet a million dollars she knows more about Otto than she said this morning."

I start to walk away, and Amber calls to me. "You seriously aren't going to help? I thought we were partners!"

We can't be partners. Not on *Odyssey,* and not with my Special Service assignment. Gran will kill me if she finds out I've involved Amber at all.

Not smart to give Amber a chance to argue, so I keep moving. "Sorry, Amber. I have to quit *Odyssey.*"

Whatever she says in response is muffled by the buzz of kids eating lunch, but I can't worry about it. I need to find Comcast Man.

I work backward, scouring each exit and then the aisles between the long tables. Nothing. Then I move to the large picture windows, and that's where I see him. He's outside, heading in the direction of the dorms at a quick jog.

In a flash I'm out the door, scrambling past picnic tables littered with kids absorbed in their books and conversations. If they notice me rushing by, nobody says anything.

I break into a run and then remember Kyle doesn't live in the dorms. What if I'm being a supreme idiot right now? I mean, the man's here to repair the Internet, and there's Internet all over this campus. Why wouldn't he go to the dorms?

But I remember what Gran said: Jones and Brick found a camera on one of the light posts, facing the dorm entrance. And there was a mysterious man hanging around who vanished into the woods.

All the government agencies assigned to SB have missed somebody on the inside. It makes sense that that somebody is the cable repairman, but how did he pass two background checks?

As fast as my legs will go, I follow the line of trees that stretch along the school's eastern perimeter until I round the last bend and the dorm is in sight. A Comcast truck is straddling the grass edge of the drive. He parked up here?

My eyes flit from the mostly empty lot, over the island of grass and benches and pruned trees in front of the entrance, to the dorm building in front of me—but there's nothing, and nobody. I slink along a row of boxwood shrubs that line the side of the dorm, panting, trying to control my breathing.

Where the heck did he go? Where should I go?

There's a row of golf carts parked in minispaces, and

I crouch between the two closest to the dorm entrance. Maybe I should find a way to get inside—I could try swiping my student ID.

I've started to move when there's a rustle to my left, and my chest hardens like a piece of granite. I can't swallow, or breathe or move at all; every cell in my body is frozen, stiff with fear.

And then Comcast Man starts talking. But not to me.

"Yeah. Definitely. The secretary said there's been five this year. I'm getting the other camera now."

Five? Five what? The guy is definitely up to something. After a few seconds of silence, I twist my body a fraction of an inch at a time, until I can see him standing in the grass, a phone to his ear. I pray he doesn't look my way as I work my SpiPhone out of my pocket. I don't have time to go to the Special Service side, so I hit the video on my regular home screen and angle the phone toward Comcast Man, who's started pacing back and forth, less than ten feet away from me.

When he speaks again, he sounds irritated. "No, I've double-checked everything, nobody can trace me—or you. It's all stand-alone, and once I get the memory cards to you...Uh-huh. But this job is a pain in the neck. Anything else will cost you big. Security is off the charts."

More silence. Then, "Yeah. I can get inside. But like I said, if you want one on each floor it'll be expensive. I'm risking my job. I'll meet you in the same place. Give me twenty minutes and I'll hand over what I've got so far."

And then he's on the move, walking right past me, away from the dorm entrance. He doesn't look back, and I force my legs, my whole body, to rise—and keep recording as he approaches his truck and slides a ladder off the top. He gives a quick look around as he crosses the blacktop to the light post on the center island, directly across from the dorm entrance.

I watch him climb the ladder and fool with something. It's got to be the camera Jones and Brick found last night. It has to be. I zoom in. Whatever it is, he's taking it, and he'll probably give it to the person he was talking to on the phone.

My hand starts to tremble, making it impossible to keep the phone steady.

Forget it. I have enough. I look down at the screen and name the video *COMCAST MAN NABS CAMERA*, and then I send the file to Gran and the captain.

By the time I look up again, Comcast Man is climbing down the ladder. Shoot. He's gonna leave. What if that camera footage helps the bad guys get Kyle?

There's no way Gran can get somebody here in time, not if he's gonna meet the person on the other end of the phone. Dang it. Dang it. Dang it.

I have to stop him.

I look around as Comcast Man struggles to put the ladder back on his truck. There's only one way to do this, but I'm going to look like a total blockhead. At best.

I hop into the closest golf cart and turn the key, thanking Gramps in my head for letting me drive him around the golf course on Saturday mornings.

In an instant I've got it in forward gear and the pedal to the floor. I crank the steering wheel right-left-right, so that the cart whips back and forth in a wackadoo zigzag. Comcast Man is thirty feet away and closing, coming around the back of his truck, his eyes wide at the sight of me.

I aim in the general direction of the tips of his shoes, 'cause actually killing the guy would be a bad idea. But then my foot gets caught somewhere between the acclerator and the brake at the exact same moment I hit a bump and give the steering wheel one more crank.

The golf cart jumps the bump, tips hard to the left and rolls sideways on two wheels toward the truck and Comcast Man, who's waving his arms in a panic, yelling obscenities, trying to get me to stop. Only, the cart is out of control and I can't stop.

The golf cart teeters on its side and closes in on Comcast Man in terrifyingly slow motion. There are two things I know for sure as I lean right in a last-ditch effort to not fall out of the cart and to get the other two wheels back on the ground: first, I'm gonna hit way more than the tips of Comcast Man's shoes. And second, there's another visit to Headmistress Williams's office in my near and unfortunate future.

And just like that, the golf cart crashes against the truck and traps Comcast Man, who's now screaming bloody heck, telling me to get the stupid hunk of metal off him. Like I'm Iron Man or something.

There's only one thing for an underage underachieving undercover agent to do. I pick up my SpiPhone and call 911.

# 17

The ambulances, the police cars, the fire trucks, the army of agents from the school and Gran and the captain, dressed as their real-life selves, all show up within sixty seconds of each other. Gran orders somebody to wrap special violet-colored tape around the entire accident scene, which includes the light post and the dorm entrance, until her people can get there. Which means *nobody* crosses it without her say-so or the president of the United States will shout something like "Off with their heads!"

Apparently the area is now a high-level crime scene and POTUS says she's in charge. The police are upset, Kang is pacing mad, and Headmistress Williams is standing helpless on the sidelines of the whole spectacle, majorly confused. But nobody is confused when I get pulled into a private room to be interrogated.

I grin at Gran as the captain closes the door. "Did you see the video?"

"Clayton, I have no idea what you're talking about. The file you sent was blank." I know my grandmother won't kill me, despite the number of lethal weapons hidden under her skirt, but the expression on her face tells me the thought has recently crossed her mind. "What have we said, again and again? Your orders are to stick with Kyle. *Only* Kyle. Didn't Captain Thompson remind you of that last night? And I gave you specific orders to do just that less than an hour ago."

I feel a sharp burn rush up my neck as she continues. "Do you realize the mess you've made? This little incident has forced me to get the Special Service involved in this entire business front and center. All to protect your identity."

Captain Thompson doesn't say anything. He doesn't have to; I can tell he's as disappointed in me as Gran is. I have to make them understand: Comcast Man is bad. "But the cable guy, I heard him on the phone. He's up to something, Gran. I swear it. And he was taking down the camera on the light post, the one Jones and Brick found. Why would he do that if he wasn't in on whatever's going on around here?"

"All I can say is, thank the good Lord you didn't kill the poor man. And don't you worry. He'll be thoroughly checked out *now*. But Clayton Patrick Stone, from now on you need to follow orders. Exactly. Is that clear?"

I nod. What else can I do?

Gran closes her eyes and is still for a moment. Captain Thompson opens the door, like he knows we're finished, and at the sound Gran opens her eyes and gestures for me to get moving. "We need to have a chat with your headmistress."

Headmistress Williams is waiting beyond the crime tape. Gran shakes the headmistress's hand and explains the cover story she never told me. I know better than to argue. "From my interview with him, I understand this young man was looking around the dorms on his lunch break because he's thinking about living in them next year. When he realized the time, he borrowed a golf cart so he wouldn't be late for his next class, which led to this mishap. Fortunately for us, he inadvertently pinned a person my agency has been watching in connection with a highly sensitive case."

Gran gestures to the utility trucks pulling up behind her. "Please report that there has been a gas leak and declare this area off-limits to all staff and students. We'll need about two hours to collect evidence and will send word after we've cleared the premises." She leans in toward the headmistress confidentially. "I hope you understand that this incident never happened, and if word gets out, we will bring criminal charges against the source."

Headmistress Williams mumbles her agreement. I wouldn't argue with my grandmother, either. Not when she's doing her job, at least.

Gran briefly places her hand on my shoulder. "Now, would you mind making sure this young man gets settled into class with a proper excuse? We need to avoid any questions or speculation, but I want you to know, he has been instrumental in helping his country today."

And then she's gone, dismissing me and Headmistress Williams. We have our orders; it's back to school as if nothing happened.

I'm in a daze for the next hour as I try to shake off all my ridiculous mistakes. I gotta get it together, or Kyle is doomed. So I do the undercover look-over-his-shoulder move every three minutes as we switch classes. I mean, who knows when dudes with hats and guns are gonna pop out of a closet to carry out some sort of international kidnapping plan?

It takes till health class before I'm less bummed about my golf cart disaster and start to notice a different kind of chatter than Gran and the captain are worried about—posted with whispers instead of keyboards. All over the school kids are talking about Peter's dad in the news. And Amber was right: there's a definite rumor that Peter is dropping out of the election.

There's not a doubt in my mind that Otto has something to do with the rumors going around SB—in fact, that he has something to do with everything—but I do my best to ignore all the gossip and keep focused on Kyle like Gran ordered, even though I still feel sorry for Peter.

Whether the buying votes thing is true or not, it can't be fun to see headlines about your dad splashed all over the Internet like that, especially at a school like SB.

There's one good thing about Peter's drama: my craziness from yesterday is already old news. Even some of the lacrosse dudes are saying "Hey" when they pass me in the hall, and by the time the final bell rings, I realize I'd actually be looking forward to lacrosse practice if it weren't for Otto.

I push through the locker room doors thirty seconds behind Kyle and pass the suits already positioned in the usual places. I hesitate as I approach Kang, fingering the presidential pen, still in my pocket from this morning. I should give it back to him. Gramps has a couple in his attic office. He even framed one of them because it meant so much to him. I stare up at the man half a second too long.

"Move it, kid."

Obviously now's not the right time for a meaningful

conversation. I slide past him to my side of the bench, so conveniently situated next to Kyle's. "Hey," I say when our eyes meet.

Kyle nods back at me and keeps getting dressed. I open my locker and have started pulling stuff out when I hear a snort like stifled laughter. A warning tingle travels down my spine. Laughter or not, that didn't sound right.

I put my cleats on the bench and move past Kyle to the other side of the lockers. There're a couple of guys on the next row, nothing going on. It's the next set of lockers where I find them.

James is sitting on the bench, looking at an empty locker, a blank expression on his face. And Otto is standing, fully dressed for practice, in a bent-over position, red from laughter.

"What's up?" I ask. I really don't care who answers.

James looks up and shakes his head. "Don't worry about it."

Otto grins in a way only he could. "Yeah, don't worry about it."

I scan the area for a hint about what's going on. Guys are wandering past in various stages of getting ready, but nobody's paying attention to us.

Otto has obviously done something to mess with James. I finally realize what it is: James's locker is empty, and he's still wearing his school uniform.

"Where's his stuff, Otto?"

Otto looks from James to me and smirks. "I have no idea what you're talking about." Then he shuts his locker and disappears around the corner. A second later I hear the clang of the exit door.

"I think I know where he put them." The voice comes from behind me, and I turn to see Kyle. "He's not particularly original when it comes to pranks."

Kyle moves to Otto's locker and opens the one beside it. Sure enough, there's a rumpled pile of practice gear, complete with cleats. Kyle hands the pile to James. "It's not you. He can't help himself."

I want to say something like *What? He can't help being a jerk?* But Kyle just did something cool, despite the fact that he and Otto are technically friends, so I keep my mouth shut.

"Thanks," says James, taking the clothes. "Back in my old school I would have made him pay for that. Actually, he never would have gotten this far with me at home."

Kyle and I look at each other and then back at James. That has to be the most that's come out of his mouth, ever. Or at least since I've known him.

James takes off his shirt, and I'm confused all over again. The way he acts does not match up with his skills on the lacrosse field, or his totally-beyond-seventh-grade muscles. The only middle school guys I've seen who look like that with the chiseled arms and stomachs are gymnasts or wrestlers. Of all people, I'm thinking James could stand up to Otto—if he wanted to.

Kyle raises his eyebrows. "You know, Coach doesn't play you because you don't take Otto on—I mean, on the field. You might want to think about giving it a hundred percent out there."

Until this moment, I've been on the fence about Kyle. Amber says he's a decent guy, but this is the first real evidence I've seen to back that up. Maybe he would be a good friend. I mean, if all this were real.

"Yeah, James," I say. "Yesterday I saw you weasel out of dealing with him at practice, which took some pretty respectable footwork." I shoot Kyle another look before adding, "But a guy like Otto only sees that as running. Why don't you stand your ground?"

One of the defensive guys appears and opens the locker next to James's.

James throws him a brief glance, then turns back to Kyle and me with a shrug. "Trust me, I would if I could." He shakes his head. "I just can't."

Kyle's security detail surrounds us as Kyle, James and I make our way to the field, Kang taking the rear. There are more suits than usual; it makes me remember what Gran said earlier in the janitor's closet about the messages online and the fact that the lacrosse team was mentioned. They have Comcast Man in custody. Maybe they found out something when they interrogated him. Whatever is going on now, it's more serious.

We drop our bags, slip across the sideline and join the rest of the team, sticks in hand. James holds his up for a catch as he lopes across the turf. I scoop a ball and toss it to him, and we start to send it back and forth. My eyes run the length of the field. Suits are positioned every twenty yards or so, a few feet back from the sidelines, some of them facing out, some facing the field. Kyle has found a partner closer to the midline. He isn't throwing with us, but he's not with Otto, either.

The sunshine, the cool breeze and the balls flying make me miss Toby and everyone at Masters. They're probably wondering where I am, but they also knew I could disappear without warning, so I doubt they're freaking out.

Last night, right before I went to sleep, I got a text from Toby, and one from Laci, too. Toby's said, **I'll keep bringing mocha in case you show**. Laci's said, **Be safe**.

Coach blows his whistle and calls us to the center of the field.

It's gotten seriously busy since we walked out of the locker room, and most of the other SB fields are full—people everywhere.

The Sydney Brown girls' lacrosse players are practicing on their field, which is inside the track where the SB runners are doing timed sprints and jumping hurdles. To the south, the baseball team is getting ready for a game—I squint to figure out who the opponent is, but I can only see the color of the jerseys: crimson and white.

Coach holds up his clipboard and blows the whistle. In an instant, all eyes are on him as he talks about tomorrow's game. Today he's splitting us up into four groups: two will scrimmage against each other, one will run drills—and those three groups will alternate. The fourth group will work on face-offs.

Then he calls out four names and I hold my breath until he says "Max Carrington." Otto was right, I did make it.

As Coach divides the rest of the players, I spot Mr. Harvard.

Unfortunately for me, he made the face-off cut, too.

There are two guys standing next to him, and I figure

they're the other two—I remember them from yesterday's drills. I walk over and stick out my hand. "Hey, I'm Max."

The guy on the end takes my hand. "I'm Matt," he says as he nods to the other guy. "This is Carlson."

Otto chuckles. "You do realize we're not in this together. We're working against each other. You know, *facing off*? See who wins?"

Before I can think of an answer, Coach claps Otto on the back as he walks by. "You boys follow me."

Carlson and Matt immediately jog after Coach.

"Sure thing, Coach," says Otto. He snaps the strap on his helmet and grins. "You show up at the end of the year, make a fool of yourself *saving* Kyle from a lockdown, and then step onto this field like you own the place. Trust me, Max Carrington, your days are numbered. I'll make sure you end up just like Peter. You won't even see it coming. Nobody ever does."

I stare back at Otto. He can't be for real. He's basically admitting that he wants Peter to drop out of the election.

Sort of stunned, I follow Otto across the field to where Coach is waiting. I've never met someone who can threaten you with a smile plastered on his face.

I reboot my brain and force myself to pay attention to Coach, who's already talking.

"...So this is an important position, and as of right now, our plan is to alternate each of you into Wednesday's game and see who works best. Max, you did well enough yesterday to get to this point, but as of right now, you're unproven on the field. What's your usual position again?"

"Attack."

"Attack. And you're a lefty? You ever play midfield?" I can feel his doubt, big-time.

I nod and scramble for an answer. Something that will make him take me seriously. "Yes, sir. Whenever necessary. My grandfather was a college coach. He made sure I knew every position and forced me to play with both hands."

"Oh," Coach says. He cocks his head and takes a long look at me. "That helps."

I let out the breath I've been holding, a little relieved. I hope it really *does* help. I need to move out of last place.

Gramps taught Toby and me face-off basics a few months before he died; he said we needed to be prepared for anything and made us go against each other in the backyard. I'm a lefty, so it was crazy frustrating, 'cause I have to do it the same way as the other guys. Gramps drilled me hard, but since Percy has always been the face-off specialist for our team, I never got a whole lot of real game practice.

"So we're going to be drilling you four against each other for the next two hours. Repetition is key. I'm not expecting any of you to be FOGOs, but by the end of practice today you'll have a favorite grip and stance, and hopefully start to notice your opponent's strengths and weaknesses and begin to adjust to them. Any questions?"

Sheesh. It's real nice he doesn't expect us to magically turn into Face-Off Get-Offs in one day. I mean, those guys are only on the field for face-offs; they're obviously the *best*.

When we don't say anything, Coach steps back. "Okay, we've got to be ready for the game tomorrow, let's get started." He gestures toward Otto and me. "You two first."

The other pair watches as Coach places the ball on the

ground. He holds the whistle near his mouth and waits for me and Otto to push the mesh of our pockets inside out and face each other on opposite sides of the midline.

"Down," he says, the whistle between his lips.

We both crouch low, positioning our sticks and bodies so we're ready to react. I'm hyperaware that Otto's knee is on the ground—and mine's not.

Coach crouches with us, hands on his knees, watching for any mistake, making sure our sticks are lined up. He places the ball and then backs off.

"Set."

From here out we can't move or touch the ball until he blows the whistle. I know this like I know the grass is green and the sky is blue, but in the three quarters of a second between him backing off and the whistle, I lurch forward.

Coach shakes his head. "Max, you jumped the ball. You just gave Otto's team possession. Let's try again."

Otto smirks. He takes a breath, ready to make some sort of obnoxious comment, but Coach sends him a warning look and Otto closes his mouth.

We repeat the sequence, and this time I'm more careful, telling myself: Do not so much as flinch. The whistle blows and Otto clamps down on the ball, securing it under his head. I come forward with my shoulder, attacking Otto and his stick, trying to free the ball before he can get completely upright.

I feel Coach and the other guys take a few steps back, not wanting to get caught up in the rumble. Miraculously, the ball pops loose and rolls behind Otto, giving me the advantage: I can see it and go after it in one forward motion. I scoop the ball and sprint downfield until Coach blows the whistle.

I jog back and toss the ball to Coach. He gives me a satisfied nod. "Not bad," he says. "But we have a lot of work to do." He points to the other guys. "Your turn."

I step back to give them room and catch Otto giving me his death stare. If he didn't like me after Peter's interview, he hates me now.

Two hours of facing off against Toby in the backyard with Gramps blowing the whistle and making the calls is one thing. But it's another world with Coach Pearce on the Sydney Brown midline.

We go at it steadily, taking turns, switching opponents, with Coach making us pay attention to different stuff every single time: reverse grip; motorcycle grip; knee down; standing position; stick position; clamping; raking; kicking the ball; spidering; using your shoulders, knees and feet; and all the legal and illegal moves in the midst of the whole face-off operation. In the end, whatever battle is going on between Otto and me has helped us both get better—of the four of us, it's pretty clear we've earned the top two spots, at least in Coach's mind.

But rivalry comes at a cost, and by the time practice is over I'm dragging myself to the sidelines. My body is a wreck, and so is my brain, so it takes a couple of minutes before I snap out of my zone and actually *see* the other guys—and remember Kyle and James.

Holy mother of zero visibility. Anything could have happened in the past couple of hours and I would have been totally out of it. I didn't check on Kyle the entire time. Not even once.

Hunched over my bag, I look around at the guys in various states of leaving for home. Some downing water and Gatorade, others gathering their stuff and heading back to the locker room, or the waiting cars and limos in the parking lot. It's easy to spot Kyle in the middle of it all.

I pick up my gear and have started to walk his way when Otto swoops in and claps Kyle on the back. He says something and they both laugh, and then Otto holds out his hand. Kyle hesitates for a moment, but then he puts his out and shakes with a quick nod. I guess they're friends again. Amber will be delighted to hear *that*.

"Max?"

James is standing beside me. I put my eyes back on Kyle, who's now walking to the parking lot with Kang on his heels and three agents ahead of him. Once he gets into his mini-motorcade and is on his way to the White House, I'm free and clear.

I face James and sling my bag over my shoulder, my focus officially changed for the night. Living in the dorms, James probably hasn't had a home-cooked meal in a while. Not that he's gonna get one at my house, but if Gran wants to rule him out as a problem, maybe I can speed up the process. "James, want to come to my house for dinner?"

And for the first time since I've known him, the guy smiles.

# 18

The Special Service limo driver pulls up to the house and escorts James and me inside. It's his job to make sure everything's okay before he leaves and sits at his post down the street for the rest of the night. Gran wanted at least three agents posted around the block at all times, but Captain Thompson argued long and hard that a bunch of agents—even disguised ones—would fall under *obvious*, not *undercover*.

Anyway, if James thinks it's weird that our "chauffeur" is checking out the house like he owns it, he doesn't say anything.

I'm about to ask where he wants to do homework when Captain Thompson and Gran come barreling through the front door, with loud complaints about the DC traffic. I run out of the family room and into the foyer, signaling with my finger that I'm not alone.

For a split second there's silence. Then Captain Thompson continues his rant about it taking thirty minutes to travel two miles while Gran disappears down the back hall.

The captain is back in character as my dad, Mitchell

Carrington. He raises his extra-fake-and-bushy eyebrows at me and then ambles into the family room and puts down his computer bag. I know he's thinking: Why the heck did you invite a kid here? I follow him into the room where James is waiting.

"Dad," I say, squashing down a strange feeling as the word finds its way out of my mouth. "This is James Scott. He's pretty new at school, too."

In a flash of understanding, the captain switches gears. He rubs his balding head, smiles and sticks out his other hand for a shake.

"James, it's good to meet you. I hear you're a lacrosse player."

James shakes Dad Thompson's hand. "Yes, sir, Mr. Carrington."

"So what brings you and your family to DC?"

"Uhh, my mom's job." James snatches a quick look at me, like he's asking for help.

So I interrupt. "Hey, Dad." This time "Dad" comes out a little easier. "We're gonna go up to my room until dinner's ready, okay?" I figure James won't hold up under the Special Service parental interrogation. But maybe if we're alone...

The second I close the door to my bedroom, James faces me with a desperate expression on his face. "Can I use your phone?"

I know for a fact that he has his cell phone on him right now. He used it right before we got in the limo to come home. "Yours stopped working?"

He nods. "I think it's the battery." An out-and-out lie, I can tell by the way he's looking at the floor and mumbling.

"James, seriously. What's the deal?"

He walks over to my bed and sits, his shoulders drooping as if he's lost something big, like his dog or his best friend. He lifts his head and stares directly into my eyes before he finally speaks again. "I'm not supposed to use my phone to call anybody except my mom, not even my dad. It's not safe."

About a thousand pins and needles run down my spine. *Not safe?* What does that mean? I thought something weird was going on—now I'm positive. I need to make sure it doesn't have anything to do with Kyle. Only, I can't ask that—yet. I start with the most logical question.

"What do you mean, *not safe*?"

He meets my eyes again. "Listen, it's just, my life is a mess right now. My mom's going through something and she wants to keep it private. Will you please let me use your phone? I haven't talked to my best friend for months. He doesn't even know what happened. We just left one night without telling anybody."

"You and your family?"

He shakes his head. "It's only me and my mom. My parents are divorced. Listen, Max, I shouldn't even be here—I'm supposed to be staying put in the dorm. My mom decided lacrosse would be okay, but that's it."

I clap him on the back and stand up. "Don't worry about it," I say, digging in my pocket for my cell phone. I make sure it's set to my regular number and hand it to him. "Call your bud. I'll wait for you downstairs."

I walk out the door, and as I start to pull it closed, I think about leaving it cracked so I can listen to whatever he has to say. But I can't do it. James isn't my friend, exactly, but he's not my enemy, either.

I pull the knob till I hear the latch click into place, and then slowly walk down the stairs.

I enter a completely different kitchen from last night. Gran is tearing lettuce leaves, eyeing a bubbling pot of red sauce on the stove, while Captain Thompson has his sleeves rolled up, both hands deep inside a mixing bowl, kneading and squeezing with a miserable look on his face. I can't quite tell if it's pain from his shoulder or disgust at touching raw meat.

I stand in the doorway and watch Gran set her salad aside and step closer to the captain. She folds her arms and inspects over his shoulder.

Captain Thompson stops squeezing and crooks his neck as he eyes her suspiciously. "I don't understand why I can't use a spoon. Or what about one of those electric mixing thingamajigs?"

Gran gives him the same patient look she'd give a three-year-old as she explains. "You are not simply stirring, *Mitchell*. You are fusing the pork, beef, egg, bread crumbs, cheese, garlic and all the rest, so that when you take one bite, you taste it all. That takes the love of your hands, not a spoon—or a thingamajig."

It's hard not to smile as I remember my own meatball lesson from a few years ago, only it was my dad who taught me. Both my parents were pretty awesome cooks, and now I know why. Gran wouldn't have it any other way. It makes me feel proud—of all of them.

She looks up and sees me, her eyes traveling beyond where I stand, checking for James. *Where is he?* she mouths, stepping back from the captain.

I point upstairs and whisper, "On the phone."

She nods and turns to the captain. "Mr. Carrington, why don't you go get changed and let me finish this?"

She doesn't have to ask twice. Without another word, "Dad" is at the sink, washing meat goop off his hands. With a quick wink to me, he hightails it out of the kitchen and disappears down the hall.

I walk up to Gran, and she gives me a brief hug. "It's been a while since we had a real family dinner, hasn't it?"

"Yeah," I say, trying to sound happy. To *be* happy.

"I know," she says with a tiny smile. "It's not easy for me, either. And I'm sorry for getting so upset with you today. You need to know that I'm thankful every day that you and I still have each other, and even though I miss your grandfather, and your parents, I believe they are still with us."

She's right. I still hear them in my head all the time. I wonder if that will ever stop.

She gives my shoulders another squeeze before getting back to business. "Do we need to discuss what happened today, or are we clear?" she says as she rolls up her sleeves and reties her apron.

"We're clear. And I'm sorry. But I really think there's something going on with the Comcast dude. I had video to prove it."

Gran's voice is hushed when she finally speaks. "We've got him isolated, and I have people checking his home as a precaution. But Clayton, you must realize you are a young man dealing with a grown-up situation. Your job is a tiny piece of this puzzle."

It sounds like she doesn't believe me. "Did you check his phone? I told you I heard him talking to somebody."

Gran's eyes bulge, and in an instant, the knuckles that were about to dig into Captain Thompson's meatball ingredients take a detour and snag my shirtsleeve. Before I know it, she's pulled me into the pantry and the door is shut behind us.

She lets out an exasperated sigh. "You must remember to keep your voice down, Clayton. There is currently an outsider in the house."

"Sorry, I didn't mean to—"

Gran speed-talks right over my apology. "We found the cable person's work phone. There were no calls—incoming or outgoing—of consequence, but we're still attempting to track any cellular activity from that location at that time. Oh, and we have the cameras, but the memory cards are missing." Her eyes flit to the closed door and then to me.

"Since we're here, quickly tell me," she says, "what have you found out about James?"

I shake my head. "Gran, I don't think he's anything to worry about, but something is definitely up. He can't talk to anybody but his mom on his phone, not even his dad, because he says it's not safe. He wasn't making any sense. Oh, plus his parents are divorced."

"Ah," she says, her shoulders relaxing, "this is beginning to make sense. It sounds like a custody problem, and perhaps involves something we're not aware of—a threat of some kind. If that's the case, then James and his mother might have a good reason to hide."

"You mean a threat from his dad?"

Gran purses her lips and stares at me a moment. "Unfortunately, this happens. And it would explain why there is no record of them. It appears that they've been very careful, cutting ties not only with his father, but with his father's friends and family. Depending on the situation, sometimes the only way to stay safe is to completely disappear."

I think I hear footsteps on the floorboards upstairs and gesture toward the ceiling to alert Gran. She nods back at me, keeping her voice low. "I'll try to confirm this on my end, but it may prove difficult, as organizations work very hard to protect families dealing with this type of problem."

Then she slowly cracks the door open and peers into the kitchen. "We're clear," she whispers, grabbing a can of tomatoes. And then more loudly as we walk across the room and back to the counter, "It's always in the last place you look. Thank you for helping me, Max."

She scoops a handful of ground meat from the bowl and begins to roll a meatball. "Max," she says as James enters the room, "dinner will be ready in an hour. You and James can use the kitchen table to work on your homework until then."

Figures. Even when she's working undercover as a housekeeper, my grandmother would never forget about homework.

# 19

The next morning at breakfast I'm still thinking about the whole James thing. We finished our homework after dinner, and then our agent disguised as a limo driver took him back to the dorm. I got the feeling James would rather have stayed with us, though. He said it was nice being part of a family again.

Yeah. Same here. I even started wondering what it would be like to have a brother.

I mean, I don't know exactly what the deal is, but if it's as serious as Gran says, I'm thinking James might need somebody to look out for him.

I swallow a bite of scrambled eggs and clear my throat. "James seems scared about whatever's going on with his family. Do you think we should be protecting him, too?"

Captain Thompson chokes so hard a Cheerio flies out of his mouth, and Gran's fork stops in midair on its way to her mouth.

Gran is the first to speak. "Clayton," she says, placing her fork back on her plate. "It's difficult for me to believe we need to repeat this conversation. Kyle is your first, *and only,* priority. With the amount of intelligence chatter bouncing around, *Kyle* is the one who's dealing with a serious threat."

"But remember? You said the lacrosse team was mentioned in all that online stuff. James is on the lacrosse team, too."

Gran rolls her eyes and shoots an *It's your turn* look to Captain Thompson. He's less stern but just as insistent. "Whatever is going on with James, I'm sure it's being taken care of by the appropriate agency. If we can't find any background on him, nobody can. Whoever is handling his family's situation is doing a fine job."

"Yes," says Gran, softening her tone, "and I can't blame the boy for being scared. He's alone, and his mother is probably doing her best to create a new life for the two of them. It can't be easy. And I'm sure James loves his father, despite the difficulties." She shakes her head sympathetically. "No, it can't be easy for either of them."

Captain Thompson pushes his chair back and stands. "But as long as James is not a threat to Kyle—and from what I can tell, *he's not*—then he has nothing to do with your job at Sydney Brown." He picks up his cereal bowl and looks me in the eyes. "Clayton, this is the difficult part of working undercover. You must understand that the people you meet and interact with are important only as it relates to your job. And your job is to become friends with and stay close to Kyle Hampton. That's it. Everything you do, every person you get to know at Sydney Brown, should fuel *that* mission, nothing else. Don't try to make it more complicated."

The conversation is over. "Yes, sir."

A couple of minutes later, Captain Thompson leaves the kitchen and Gran leans over her empty plate. "By the way, is it getting better with Kyle?"

I look back at her. "Yeah. He's talking to me now. Actually, he's not bad."

Gran sits back and smiles. "I knew you could do it."

I swallow my last bite of eggs and take my plate to the sink. Gran does not understand how complicated my life has become.

James and Kyle are all I think about on the ride to school. I get what Gran and the captain are saying, especially after my screw-up yesterday. But I don't see a problem. I can keep an eye on both Kyle and James, especially since dealing with Kyle is getting easier.

Nobody has to know.

I pass through the large main doors, where both the Stripes and the Stars have set up tables with campaign pins and stickers. Huge banners hang behind them.

The banners say things like:

DOUBLE YOUR MOCHA DOLLARS FOR A *BIGGER, BETTER* SB CAFÉ. VOTE PETER GALLAGHER!

And:

ALL SB SPORTS DESERVE EQUAL FUNDING. VOTE FOR MONIQUE BOWLING. SHE'S ON YOUR TEAM!

I don't see Monique or Peter anywhere, though. Maybe they're in the coffee lounge. I walk down the carpeted halls to my locker and notice there are twice as many election posters as yesterday.

I unload and sneak a look at Kang, who's standing guard as Kyle empties his backpack. I've decided to give the giant man back his pen, sort of as a peace offering.

I take it out of my pocket and walk past Kyle. I know Kang sees me coming, even though he doesn't move and his expression doesn't change. I stop directly in front of him and slowly extend the pen.

He looks me up and down before he speaks. "What's that?"

"Your pen. I think you dropped it."

For the first time in three days his eyebrows come together in an actual human expression. He takes the presidential pen and studies it, then shakes his head. "Nope. Not mine."

"Are you sure?"

Kang hands the pen back to me. "That's an official pen. One of the ones the president gives away after he signs a bill or an important document. You might want to turn it in, or keep it." He returns to his original and uptight position.

I put the pen in my pocket and walk away. I guess it could be anybody's, especially around this school. Only, I have a weird feeling it didn't turn up next to my locker by accident.

I head down the east hall toward the coffee bar. I need a mocha and some time to think.

"You've got guts."

I turn as Kyle falls in beside me. "What do you mean?"

"Nobody talks to Kang. Especially after ticking him off the way you did."

I laugh. "Yeah, well, he's only doing his job." Like I'm trying to do mine. "What you did yesterday, helping James even though you're buds with Otto, that was cool."

Kyle keeps his eyes straight ahead. "I think he's gone a

little overboard with James. I'm going to try to talk to him." Then he looks at me. "Don't let Otto get to you."

Too late; Otto gets to me in a big way. Time to change the subject.

"You ready for the game today?"

Kyle shrugs. "It'll be a tough one, that's for sure. What about you? Think you'll be facing off?"

We approach the coffee bar and start to slow our pace. I look at Kyle and realize that as long as Kyle and I are talking, it doesn't matter if I face off or not. "Don't know. The competition is really good."

Kyle stops and stares at me for a second. We both know I mean Otto. Then he quickly walks between the crowded campaign tables and gets into the coffee line. I follow him, glancing over my shoulder to see how many suits are in our wake. Kang's about ten feet away, and another two agents are farther back.

I remember one of the first things Gran told me about Sydney Brown. A bunch of kids have security, but none of them has to deal with it constantly the way Kyle does. He's obviously sick of it. I would be, too. Being the president's only son must be a bummer in a lot of ways. Which reminds me; I pull the ultraofficial pen out of my pocket as I catch up to him.

I hold the pen out. "Is this yours?"

Kyle takes it and examines it closely. "It's one of the pens people fight over so they can frame it and put it in their house. So stupid." He shakes his head as he hands it back. "It's not mine. I've had one or two, but I gave them away."

Before I ask, I know the answer. It's the only thing that makes sense. "Ever give one to Otto?"

"Yeah. My dad would never give one to his dad." Kyle swipes his card and then turns to me. "Why?"

"No reason," I say, swiping my card. But now I know it wasn't Kang who searched my locker, it was Otto.

We move over to a corner to wait for our drinks. There's nobody within a few feet of us, and I lean toward him. "So what's the deal with you two? You guys seem really different to be such good friends." I'm not just asking because of my job. I honestly want to know.

Kyle is completely still, and for a second, I think he's not going to answer. But he does. "We've known each other for a long time, but we've never been friends because our fathers pretty much work against each other every day." He laughs and adds, "I never thought about it before, but it's like lacrosse. Our dads are trying to do the same thing: get the ball and score. But they're on two different teams."

The barista making drinks calls us over and hands us our cups. Kyle takes his and gestures for me to follow him into the hall, where it's less crowded. He slides down the wall and sits on the carpet. I do the same.

"How did you get to be friends if your dads are rivals?"

Kyle exhales. "Nobody knows this." He looks directly at me and hesitates for a moment before going on in a whisper. "See, Otto helped me out of a bad situation—something I couldn't tell anybody about."

"Bad situation?"

I wait. This might be why Kyle started acting weird around his dad, and around SB.

Kyle scans the hallway, as though what he has to say is top secret. I can barely hear him when he speaks. "Otto got rid of proof that I cheated on a test. And then somehow the teacher who was going to accuse me resigned. I don't know for sure, but I think Otto or his dad had something to do with that, too." He closes his eyes, and I can feel his regret. "I never cheated in my whole life until that one time. We'd just gotten back from a trip to China, and I was so tired, and...I don't know. Like I said, it was stupid, and I wish I could go back in time and change what I did. All of it."

Duh. He owes Otto. Questions are popping like rocket fire in my mind. I want to ask him about Peter, and the election, and—everything. But then the bell rings, and we both scramble to our feet and join the rush to first period.

As we hurry down the hall, I'm starting to get why Kyle is friends with Otto. Kyle is a nice—and loyal—guy. And in this case, that's the problem.

Otto isn't gonna protect anybody unless he has something to gain. So the real question is, what is it that Otto wants? And what is he willing to do to get it?

# 20

I make it all the way to third-period English feeling better about the job I'm doing. Yesterday was the pits, but today's not bad. Gran and Captain Thompson want me to stay close to Kyle? Check. Become friends with him? Getting there. Figure out why he's quiet at the dinner table? Definitely starting to have an idea.

I'm not quite finished patting myself on the back when Amber storms into class, marches to Mr. Tatum's desk and waves her hands in the air, whispering melodramatically. The class can't understand what she's saying, but we all get the idea: she's more than a little upset.

Amber finally stops ranting and folds her arms expectantly as she stares down our English teacher.

"Er, Max Carrington and Kyle Hampton, would you please come here?" he says finally.

Kyle and I exchange doubtful glances as we approach Mr. Tatum's desk. I think we're both reluctant to step into the middle of whatever Amber's got brewing.

Mr. Tatum looks from Amber to Kyle and me. "There've been too many issues with the election this year, and we need all hands on deck. It's time to investigate both parties and make sure this election is managed fair and square." Then he zeroes in on Kyle. "Kyle, I know you've stepped back from the Stars to work for the Stripes. You've also taken time off from *Odyssey*. That means you're in a unique position to share what you know about both sides. *If* you can manage to be impartial, you might be able to help the situation."

Kyle hesitates a moment too long, and Amber faces him, her arms still folded. "You have a problem with that?"

Kyle steps back. "I don't know what you're all crazy about this time, Amber. *Nothing* is going on. But sure, I'll help if I can."

Amber lets a long whistle of steam out through her nose, and her arms fly into the air in a fed-up gesture. "Follow me," she says as she spins and heads to the door.

I start to go after her but then turn to see Kyle roll his eyes at Mr. Tatum, and Mr. Tatum mouth a definite but silent *Go* back to him.

Whatever is going on between Amber and Kyle is more than an argument about this election. They're in the middle of a tug-of-war—only, it's not rope they're pulling.

Amber leads us to the end of the west hall, down a stairwell and outside, the soft echo of Kyle's security detail reminding me that the guy's never alone.

Kyle and I stand in the sunshine and stare at each other, wondering what to do. There are a picnic table and some Adirondack chairs a few steps away.

Amber points to the table. "Sit."

We do what she says, but sheesh. "What happened, Amber? Why are you so mad?"

Kyle seems baffled, too. "Yeah. I mean, you're acting like somebody died or something."

She stares at Kyle. "Do you know what your *friend* Otto did this morning?"

"No, what?"

She narrows her eyebrows. *"Really?* Well, let me tell you." The doubt in her voice is hard to miss. "We were supposed to be working on our final projects in Spanish. Señorita Daly left the room and Otto decided to bring up Peter's dad's problem in front of everybody. At first Peter stuck up for his dad, but you know Otto. He kept interrupting him, saying the whole thing is an embarrassment for the Stripes." She takes a breath but quickly continues as she paces back and forth in front of us. "Finally Peter left, completely humiliated. But that's not all. One of the kids asked Otto if Peter was still going to run, and do you know what Otto said?" Amber's face is a furious shade of ruby red as she looks back and forth between Kyle and me. "Any guesses? Kyle, you should know. You and Otto basically *are* the Stripes' mascots these days."

Kyle shakes his head. "Are you kidding? How am I supposed to know what Otto said, or about any of this, when I wasn't there?"

Amber is not convinced. "He said that the Stripes don't need a candidate with that kind of black mark, and that he's prepared to take Peter's place."

I know surprise when I see it, and Kyle is shocked.

*"What?"* he says, starting to stand up. Then he sits back down.

"You heard me," says Amber. "Otto is taking over."

"No, he's not," says Kyle. But it sounds as if he's trying to convince himself, not us. "He's just running his mouth."

Amber sinks to the bench and turns to Kyle. She's losing steam, and she's anything but happy. "Even though all this bothers me, this is Otto being Otto." Her voice is missing the energy of a minute ago. "What I want to know is, why *you* stopped being *you*, Kyle."

Kyle flinches as if she hit him. "What do you mean?"

Amber shakes her head, and then she speaks, very, very slowly. "Kyle, we've been friends forever. But since you started hanging out with Otto, it's like you're a different person. Are you with the Stripes because of Otto? To annoy your dad?"

For a split second Amber and Kyle are fused together by some invisible thing. And then, whatever it is, it's gone, and there's a defiant spark in Kyle's eyes as he answers. "I am my own person, Amber. Just because my dad doesn't get along with Otto's dad doesn't mean we have to be the same way."

"You're right," she agrees. "But elections should be about issues, not what party people belong to or how much power their parents have. Both Peter and Monique have very good ideas. Why can't we make the SB election about those ideas instead of whether someone is a Star or a Stripe?"

He snorts back at her, and I swear it's Otto I hear, not the Kyle I talked to before school this morning. "You, of all people, know that's not the way it works in the real world, Amber."

She stands and stares at him. "So I guess you're

supporting Otto," she says, the spark back in her voice. "After all, Stripes support Stripes, right?"

Uh-oh.

Kyle takes a deep breath before he answers. "It's complicated."

With a tiny screech, she pushes away from the table and marches to the door. As she opens it, she turns back. "I'm going to find Peter. I suggest you find Otto—he probably needs help with the campaign, since there's not much time before the election." Then she faces me. "Max, are you coming?"

I casually glance around. Kang and his henchmen are posted around us in a near-and-far star pattern. I'm not sure what I *should* be doing, but somebody needs to stay with Amber until she calms down. Right now she's about two degrees of separation from becoming a danger to the president's son.

I send an apologetic look to Kyle, and he shrugs back at me.

No explanation necessary; I get "complicated."

The whole time Amber's whisking from hall to hall, searching all the hidden lounges and bathrooms for Peter, I'm reminding her that I'm no longer an *Odyssey* staff member, and that she can't drag me around like I'm her assistant. For the millionth time, I've got a job to do. In fact, I should have stayed with Kyle.

At the mention of Kyle, she simultaneously snorts and stops in her tracks. "First, *he* is part of the problem. He let this happen. Second, you're not my assistant. You're my partner." Then she grabs me and barrels forward with a solid grip on my arm, yanking me with her as she makes an unexpected hard left. "Now let's check the west wing again."

Girls.

All the running around doesn't do any good. We can't find Peter anywhere, and he doesn't answer the dozen and a half texts Amber has sent. I know this is more than a "story" to Amber. She cares about getting to the bottom of what's going on. But Peter's obviously lying low. Why would he want to talk to somebody who's only going to ask questions he doesn't want to answer?

I finally convince Amber to head back to the coffee bar, even though we've already checked it. Ever since our first pass through, I've been thinking about the glazed raspberry donut I saw in the pastry display.

I swipe my card to pay for it and join Amber at the table where she's waiting. As I take my first bite, I see Monique heading our way.

"Is it true that Peter has dropped out and Otto is going to take his place?" she immediately asks Amber.

Amber pulls out a chair for Monique. "I have no idea what's going on. I've tried to talk to Headmistress Williams, but she's in meetings all morning. She's the one who will be able to tell us if it's official news."

"I got your text yesterday, and I've been thinking about whether I should share this or not." Monique sits and takes a deep breath. "I think I know how Otto is getting kids to vote Stripes."

Amber scoots closer to Monique. "You do?"

Monique nods and holds up her cell phone. There's a picture of a kid mooning everybody out one of the school bus windows, his grinning face turned over his shoulder. I sure wouldn't want my friends or parents, or anyone, to see it. "He records kids doing stuff. Sometimes it's just embarrassing, like picking their noses, or like this." Monique points to the photo on the screen. "But sometimes it's worse. I heard he has video of a few sixth-grade girls smoking cigarettes. He'll show them the pictures or videos, and then says he'll post them on YouTube and e-mail their parents if they don't help him out with the Stripes."

Otto's words ring in my ear. He knows *everything* about *everybody* at SB. Yeah, and he uses it. There's a term for that: blackmail.

I think about the pen in my pocket. The guy will do anything to get what he wants. And then it hits me square in the chin: whether Kyle knows it or not, he's put Otto in charge of his life.

We've got to make Kyle see Otto for what he really is, but that's not all. We also have to stop this blackmail stuff he's pulling. Unfortunately, that's not going to be easy, because there's only one way to stop a guy like Otto, and that's to play the game his way. I remember the micro-video cameras Gran gave me as a consolation prize. Maybe I *can* put them to use.

I stand up. "Amber, let's go. I have an idea, but we need to find Kyle—and James."

"What are you talking about?" says Amber.

"Yeah, tell us. What idea?"

"You shouldn't get involved, Monique. Forget everything I just said and be ready to debate Peter tomorrow." It's my turn to take Amber's arm, and I pull her into the hallway as Monique looks after us with her mouth open.

"Max, what are you up to?" says Amber, dragging behind me. "Is it about Otto and the election?"

The bell rings and I pick up speed, holding tight to Amber as we dodge incoming students. "It's about *everything*," I say. And in the sixty seconds it takes to make it to the art classroom, I explain it to her.

If Kyle is still the person Amber says he was, and the person I think he is, he'll help us. I hope James will, too.

They approach from opposite directions. Amber snags Kyle, and I wave James over. There's a little nook across from the art classroom, and we land there.

"What's going on?" says James. "The bell's about to ring."

"Otto has gone too far with this election, and Max has figured out a way to stop him, if you guys will help. We need to get Otto under control."

Kyle raises his eyebrows. "I realize you don't like Otto, but when you get to know him, he's actually a good person." He sends me a meaningful look before turning back to Amber. "He honestly sticks up for his friends. But I get why you're upset. He takes politics a little too seriously."

Amber moves closer to Kyle. "Otto and honesty have nothing to do with each other. He's blackmailing kids with pictures and videos, threatening to put them on YouTube if they don't vote Stripes."

Kyle is silent for a minute, his eyes moving from Amber to James and finally landing on me. "Is this true?"

"Yes. We saw proof," I say.

The bell rings and James stands. "Whatever you want to do, count me in. I'm tired of taking it from this guy."

Amber and I get up, too, but Kyle stays put, meeting

my eyes with an uneasy expression. "You know, he never said it as a threat. He just reminded me about it, over and over again." He knows I know exactly what he's saying. He's finally put it all together and realized that, in a back-handed way, Otto is blackmailing him, too.

"There's one more thing," I say. "We think Otto's dad had something to do with leaking the story that's hurting Peter's dad." I clear my throat. It's time to tell him the thing I'm most worried about. "And that means—"

Before I have a chance, Kyle interrupts. "That means Otto's dad could do the same sort of thing to hurt my dad. And Otto wouldn't care. He's practically doing the same thing to me, in a way."

"Yeah," I say.

Kyle closes his eyes.

"Kyle?" says Amber.

He opens his eyes and looks carefully at her. "*You* know I wouldn't ever blackmail anybody."

"Of course I know that," she says. "You're a good person and a good friend—to everybody."

It seems like they both have more to say, only there isn't time.

I step toward him and offer my hand. "But Otto's *not* a friend, Kyle."

"You're right," he says as he grabs hold and stands. "So what do we do?"

"First you call Peter and convince him he still needs to run for president," says Amber with the first hint of an actual smile.

"Yep," I say, nodding my agreement. "And then we meet at lunch. This will be a play for the record books."

As of right now, I'm officially adding *Bring Otto Penrod the Third down a thousand notches* to my Special Service duties, because my assignment isn't just about mysterious bad people and all the criminal chatter surrounding SB. It's about Otto, and protecting not only Kyle, but his dad—the president of the United States.

## wednesday, may 9, 2:49 p.m.

# 21

I look at the clock on the classroom wall. It's 2:49 and last period is about to dismiss. The bus to Masters is supposed to leave at 3:30, game time 5:30.

The trap for Otto will be sprung the minute we set foot in the locker room. No, it's already been sprung. That is, if—I pull out my SpiPhone and bring up the remote camera app, crossing my fingers that James was able to set up Gran's cameras. He had like twelve minutes to get to the dorms and back without getting caught. I hit the screen a couple of times.

Yes! There it is: James's dorm room from two different angles. Huh. These *do* make me feel undercover.

At the sound of the bell, I stuff the phone back in my pocket and bolt out the door, throwing a quick glance at Kyle as I turn the corner. He's looking straight at me.

Forget the game, it's the scene in the locker room that's important right now. I hurry down the hall, silently reciting the combination Kyle gave me. Gotta move fast.

I slip into the locker room, and it's quiet. Kyle says I'll

probably have less than five minutes before anyone else shows, and he'll try to keep Otto away longer than that.

Down three rows and across, and I'm face-to-face with locker 315.

With a quick glance to either side, I start spinning the dial. Otto may be a devious overachiever in many ways, but he's also predictable, especially when it comes to choosing combinations. He's apparently used the same numbers since fourth grade: 8-23-44.

The lock gives and I pull the door open. It's all there, neatly folded like he has maid service. Come to think of it, he probably does. I only take one thing: his cleats. As an afterthought I pull the presidential pen out of my pocket and stuff it underneath the rest of his gear. No need to be obvious.

Satisfied, I shut the locker, snap the lock together and give the dial another good whirl. Then I spin around and find James's locker number. He told me the one to his left is empty. Sure enough, it's cracked open. I stuff the cleats inside and shut it hard.

I hear the clang of the main door, and with another fast look around to be sure I haven't missed anything, hustle to my own locker a couple of rows down.

By the time Kyle shows a few minutes later, I've put my gear and uniform jersey inside my bag and I'm pulling on the shooting shirt we wear for pregame travel and warm-ups. I'm pretty sure James walked by, but it's hard to know for sure, since the locker room is filling fast and getting noisy. Plus, I'm trying to stay focused and *not* turn to look every time somebody passes.

Kyle and I ignore each other as we mess with our stuff—and wait.

And wait some more.

I'm picturing what's probably, hopefully, going on two aisles down: James is sitting on his bench, getting dressed and putting his gear together. Otto is directly across from him, doing the same thing.

We're still waiting.

I flash a doubtful look at Kyle, but he just holds up his pointer finger. Yeah, I know. Be patient.

Then it happens. "Who the @&#! has my cleats?"

Bingo. I bite down on my lip and count to ten while Kyle calmly walks away, toward Otto—and James. Then I follow.

I hear slamming and banging and more cursing as I approach. And the more commotion there is, the more guys start to gather, wondering what the heck's happened.

By the time I'm next to Kyle, there are at least eight other players watching Otto's hissy fit.

James is sitting quietly on the bench. After a few seconds he turns and stares at Otto.

"What are *you* looking at?" shouts Otto.

James cocks his head with a confidence I don't think he's ever shown at SB. "I'm not looking at anything," he says. "So, your cleats are missing?"

Otto is immediately still. "What do you know about my cleats?"

James shrugs one shoulder. "I know you can't play without them." Then he stands and disappears around the corner just like Otto did yesterday.

Otto starts to chase after him, but Kyle gets a tight grip

on his arm. "Don't bother," he says. "We'll find them." He starts opening lockers until he gets to the one beside James's. "Here," he says, holding the cleats out. "Everything's good."

Otto snatches the shoes out of Kyle's hands. "Not by a long shot. Who does he think he is? That kid is going to pay."

Kyle catches my eye before answering Otto. "I'm sure he will."

That's my exit cue. Time for Kyle to innocently remind Otto that James lives in the dorms, then leave Otto to stew.

'Cause the more he stews, the faster he'll cook.

A few minutes later Coach marches through the locker room, telling us to move it. The bus is ready and he wants to beat the traffic across the bridge to Virginia. It's like a hit from behind. I'd almost forgotten, we're playing Masters Academy—my real school, and my real teammates.

I swallow hard. I can't think about that right now. I reach for my gear and head outside, where James is waiting near the bus. He nods to me and steps aboard. Everything's good so far.

I head across the blacktop and am following him up the steps when a hand lands on my shoulder. It's the bus driver.

"Gear goes in the lower compartment," he says, pointing.

Duh. "Thank you, sir." I leap back to the asphalt and toss my bag into the lower compartment. When I return to the step, the bus driver stops me again. "Good luck today," he says. Then he lowers his voice. "Watch the radar on your phone. There's lightning in the area."

I glance up to the crystal-blue sky, then take a hard look at the bearded bus driver staring back at me.

Gran—is a man?

"I'll keep an eye out," I say as I climb aboard. And as I move down the aisle of the bus, I grin something stupid. Nobody has a grandmother like mine.

Two seconds later the grin is gone. Lightning can't be good.

I sit across the aisle from James, and that's when I realize the phone Gran wanted me to check is in my lacrosse bag—I'm pretty sure the lightning thing is a metaphor for bad guys. Too bad the English test I failed last year didn't use examples that make sense. Lightning and bad guys? I get *that*.

I can only guess that Gran is telling me to stay alert. I look out the bus window and scan the parking lot. Judging by the number of black Suburbans and suits hanging around, the online postings about the lacrosse team are getting worse. That would explain why she's here undercover.

Nobody wants Kyle to disappear, that's for sure, but for the first time I'm wondering, if fifty suits with earpieces and guns can't protect him, what does the president expect *me* to do?

# 22

Chills run across my shoulders and down my body as I step off the bus and back on Masters territory as number 13, Max Carrington. Monday morning I definitely did not want to play in this game, on this field. Two days later, nothing's changed: I still don't want to play against Toby and the guys.

All the way over here my gut has been fighting me, telling me I'm in the best place to do my job—to keep an eye on things and stay close to Kyle, just in case lightning *does* strike.

I fall in line with the SB guys and take the familiar path to the field. We cross over the midline to the away team bench and drop our gear behind the benches. It's forty minutes before game time, but the stands are already filling. There are so many men and women wearing dark suits and Bluetooth ear inserts, it's kind of hard to tell who came from work to watch the game and who will shoot to kill if somebody tries to get to Kyle.

"Max!"

I recognize the voice and follow it downfield. It's

Captain Thompson, in his Dad Carrington disguise. Today he's wearing khakis and a polo shirt to go with his extra forty pounds.

I glance at Coach as I head over to "Dad," thankful he's talking to the refs. Don't need to get in trouble.

The captain claps me on the back. "Think you'll play?"

I shrug. "Don't know. Maybe it's better if I'm on the sidelines anyway, so I can watch."

The captain shakes his head. "As you can see, there's quite the security perimeter around the field and the school. What we don't have is somebody on the field within yards of Kyle. I know you might not make it on as the new guy, but if you get the opportunity, take it. And if something happens, no matter where you are, land on him fast, then get him to Agent Kang or one of us."

"You want me to watch Kyle *and* play lacrosse well enough to stay in the game?"

Captain Thompson raises his eyebrow. "Max," he says, "I'm not sure I'd pick you to simultaneously recite Latin conjugations and handle a defender, but your grandfather taught you—and me—to own the field from the second we set foot on it. And remember"—he casts his eyes across the long stretch of turf—"you know this particular field like nobody else."

In an instant it's as if Gramps is right here, telling me, like he did a million times: *The field is yours. Learn every inch of it: the ground and its bumps and divots. The goalposts and how they lean. The refs and how fast they move. Go all out against the guy you're face-to-face with, but always stay aware of every single player, back, front and sideways, your guys and your opponents. All of them. All the time.*

"Okay, it's possible, but there's something else." The Masters team is crossing the field to their bench, and I cock my head in that direction. "I'm playing against Toby and the guys. This is an important game for us, er, them. It decides how the teams are ranked for play-offs."

The captain nods. "Yes, this is difficult. But you are not betraying your Masters teammates. You're doing your job."

"Easy for you to say."

"No, it's not easy for me. I really do understand what you're going through. I know it would be easier if you weren't playing Masters, especially when you don't feel like part of the Sydney Brown team yet." He hesitates for a second before continuing. "You know that in any sport, athletes switch schools and teams all the time—whether or not they're superhero agents?"

I nod. That's true.

"Well then, try thinking about it that way. You're on a travel team and you happen to be playing against guys you know and like. But it's a game, and you have to be there for the team you're playing for—no matter what."

"So which is my team, Sydney Brown or Special Service?"

"Now you're getting it." Captain Thompson grins and claps me on the back. He starts to walk away and then turns back. "You looked good at practice yesterday. Your face-offs are coming along."

Huh. A weird feeling washes over me: he's been watching me practice. My dad used to do that, too.

I smile back at him and step onto the field. Time to go to work.

Most of our guys are tossing the ball. I scoop a grounder

and start throwing, until I notice Coach coming in our direction.

"Max, I want to talk with you," he says from a few yards away.

Coach told us on the bus that both Jeremy and Winston are still out because of their injuries, and that he'll be leaning on Otto and me for face-offs today.

I step toward him. "Yeah, Coach?"

"You did well yesterday, Max, and like I said on the bus, I want you to be ready to get on the field. But we're going to let Otto start us off."

"Yes, sir," I say, not sure why he's telling me.

"Good. Watch their man. They only have one strong specialist, so if you can figure out his moves, that'll help."

The player he's talking about is Percy. I've practiced face-offs with him. And darn it, after the way Coach worked with us yesterday, I can probably figure out a way to beat him.

I look over Coach's shoulder at my team, my old team, warming up. I could talk to them right now. Not that they'd recognize me.

Coach thumps my helmet as he walks away. "Okay, get back to warm-ups. I'm counting on you having a good game today."

I scan the Masters players as I step into the pregame drills. Captain Thompson said to think of it as if I'm playing for a travel team, so that's what I'll do: play *this* game and keep my third eye on Kyle Hampton.

I silently repeat to myself: Kyle Hampton is the reason I'm here. Kyle Hampton is the reason I'm here. And if

I need any proof of how important he is, all I have to do is look around.

I scout the field as nonchalantly as I can as I wait my turn for the drill rotation, beyond the obvious perimeter of agents who have saturated the place. Out of habit I search the stands. Amber is sitting in the front row—with Laci.

A sudden jolt hits my heart, and it races uncontrollably. What is Amber *doing*? She knows better than to say anything to Laci, doesn't she? Of course she does.

If Laci knew it was me, maybe she'd be watching me, instead of watching Toby, like she obviously is. The same way Amber is watching—who? I follow her eyes back to the SB end of the field, to the play going on now. Kyle scores, and I look back to the benches, where Amber is smiling, ear to ear.

Huh. That's interesting. She's sure keeping a close eye on him considering how much grief she's been throwing his way.

My turn next. I run into the drill, late, the ball moving fast among four of us. Somehow I hook the ball and wing it back to number 6, trying to keep my head focused on everything at once, just like Captain Thompson said, but when the ball comes back it flies past me.

I look sideways to the stands at Amber and Laci chattering away. Dang it.

This paying attention to three things at once is gonna take some work.

## weDnesDay, may 9, 5:25 p.m.

# 23

After we've run our drills and are all warmed up, Coach calls us to the sidelines and sends the captains out to talk with the refs. In groups of twos and threes, the starters from both teams begin to take their positions on the field.

It's weird being this close to my Masters teammates. A strange feeling tugs at me as I watch Toby jog to his spot—something we'd always do together.

Percy is standing at the face-off X, across from Otto, who is taller and bigger.

I watch from the sidelines, not sure what I'm hoping for. I can feel the intensity coming from both ends of the field. Every single player is focused on the two guys standing in the middle.

Percy and Otto lower themselves into position, eyes on the ball, sticks aligned. The ref bends down and makes his adjustment, then places the ball between them before backing off. I watch Percy—he's on one knee, probably so he can scramble. If Otto clamps down and sits on the ball like he usually does, Percy'll have trouble.

I take a deep breath and force myself to root for Otto.

At the same time, my eyes skim the sidelines, but the only people anywhere close are the agents standing guard. Dad Carrington and Gran the bus driver are nowhere in sight.

After a brief check on Kyle, who's waiting in the attack position, I return my attention to center, just in time for the whistle. Almost simultaneously, both sticks clamp down, trapping the ball. Percy leans into Otto with his right shoulder as they spin and struggle against each other. All at once the ball pops out, and within a second Percy's on his feet, pivoting to follow it.

It's a race. Four wingmen crash the party at full speed, and now it's a mass of bodies striking out with their sticks in a fight for possession. Percy manages to snag the ball and sends it crossfield to a waiting Dion.

They continue to zip the ball from man to man, forming an ever-tightening loop around the goal. I can tell Coach—my Masters coach—had the guys work hard on passing this week. They're fast and clean.

I hold my breath as I see the SB players try to follow the ball and prepare for the play they know is coming when, finally, Dion fakes a pass right, sending it instead to Toby, who's open and ready with a great view of the goal.

Score.

The home team fans erupt, cheering and whistling, and the Masters guys come together on the field with hugs and claps on each other's backs. I am physically restraining myself from joining them when Coach Pearce steps next to me.

"Max, get out there and tell Otto to move to left wing," he says, sounding frustrated. "You're taking this face-off."

Exactly the reality check I needed.

I hurry across the field to intercept Otto before he starts to set up. He's not gonna be happy, but—Not. My. Fault.

Otto sees me coming and his walk slows. We're about five yards away from each other when he stops. "What?"

"Coach wants you on left wing," I say.

He shakes his head but moves to the new position.

I get to the face-off X and, before I do anything else, lock in on Kyle. He's in position at right attack, probably the safest spot possible. He might be visible, but nobody can physically get to him right now. Our eyes meet and he nods. "You got this, Max!" he calls, starting a chain reaction of shouts from both sides. I hear Percy's name a couple of times, but I'm trying to put my friendships aside. He's the opponent and I've got to beat him.

The ref approaches, and it's time to concentrate: win the ball, get it to my guys. Period. "Down," he says. We both get down.

Percy's on one knee again. I know he wants to pinch and pop—we both do. I also know the direction he's leaning in. He's a good player, with fast reactions, but he always does the same thing.

The ref adjusts our sticks and then places the ball.

"Set."

He backs away and we're locked in place until the whistle. There's nothing but Percy and the ball, and I can feel my instincts kick in—not only do I need to win this ball to stay in the game, I want it. I've already decided my move: something Coach taught us yesterday.

The whistle blows, and in what seems like slow motion, I move my stick forward over the ball and jam the head of Percy's stick so he can't get to it, much less clamp down.

He's off-balance now, and in a split second I rake my stick backward, flinging the ball in the direction of Otto, who's rushing toward center. He scoops it and backpedals before moving forward again.

Now the Masters defensemen are after Otto, their sticks flailing, trying to knock the ball out of his pocket. I step back a few yards, giving Otto somebody to pass to, and as we move across the restraining line, I see Kyle out of the corner of my eye.

Otto starts to break loose from the guys who are double-teaming him, and I set a pick for him as he passes, breaking the momentum of one of his trailers. Otto puts his wheels into high gear as he heads down the sideline and whips the ball to Kyle, who's about three yards from the crease, the protected goal circle.

Immediately there are three guys whacking away at Kyle. A flag goes up, and when the ball drops, the whistle blows, and Masters defenseman Brandon gets sent to the penalty box for a slash: one minute.

Coach Pearce calls a time-out, and each team heads to the sidelines. Coach doesn't waste any time getting to the point. "We're a man up for sixty seconds. I want a score out of this. Otto, Kyle and Jay—we'll do the twenty-one triangle. Max, you don't know this play yet, so just help screen. Quick passes, and Otto, after your sixth touch, get to the three o'clock side of the crease and draw them there. Kyle or Jay, the second you've got a clear shot, let it rip. And if you don't score, recover that ball and do it again, but cut the rounds in half. Got it?"

We all respond, "Yes, sir!" and then come together with our sticks in the air and roar on three, "Sydney Brown! Huh! Huh! Huh!"

I'm heading back out, directly behind Kyle and Otto, who are leaning into each other as they walk. I think they're talking about the play—the play I've never practiced with them—when I see Kyle angrily shake his head. "Don't do it, Otto. Remember the kid you put out for the whole season?"

Otto shrugs and keeps moving. I catch up to Kyle. "What's that all about?"

He looks at me, his expression grim. "Nothing, I hope. He just doesn't like to get beat." He puts his mouth guard back in and jogs to his position.

I have a pretty good view of most of the field from my spot about five yards in front of the goal. Kyle has the ball; he's waiting for the ref to blow the whistle, with Otto about fifteen yards away. My gut is sending me warning signals. Since I met him two days ago, Otto's mood has gone from aggravated to cursing and angry.

The whistle blows, and just like Coach called, Kyle, Jay and Otto start winging the ball in a triangle pattern, with the rest of the guys running back and forth in front of the goal. I keep my eyes on Kyle, but I've got a sinking feeling as Otto cuts in and out of his route. I don't know this play, but it's obvious he's got his own agenda, and it doesn't line up with Coach's.

Otto is moving in, about three yards away from the crease, with a sideways expression. He's not looking for the ball. My eyes flit to his right, to where Percy is defending the goal, and I'm not guessing anymore. I see exactly what he's up to and I remember Otto is the guy Percy was talking about at lunch last week—the same SB player who sends kids to the sidelines, and the same one who sent a kid to the hospital. That was no accident.

I'm not close enough to stop what I see coming. In one second both Percy and Otto are on the ground. Flags fly and whistles blow. I know for a fact that Otto is the one who did the tripping with a sneaky hook around Percy's ankle, but the penalty is called on Percy, who's now limping away.

There are cheers from the SB sidelines as Percy hobbles off the field to the penalty box, barely contained anger steaming off him. He knows what happened, too.

It's not the first time I've seen a dirty play. And it's not the first time I've seen a bad call. But it is the first time I've been on this side of flat-out wrong.

Possession is given to Otto, and the whistle blows, restarting the clock. We're two men up, and the ball is flying at top speed in the same triangle formation. It doesn't take long for Kyle to see an opening and sling the ball past the goalie and into the net.

I think briefly about the cameras in James's room. Our plan needs to work, because Otto has got to be stopped. But he also has to be stopped here, on this field.

With a glance at Coach, who gives me a nod, I start to the face-off X. On my way I turn and once again make sure Kyle is in my line of vision.

I get down on one knee, eye on the ball.

The ref adjusts our sticks, moving Percy's just off the line. I keep still and wait with complete—or almost complete—focus.

At the whistle Percy is wicked fast, clamping down on

the ball a breath before I react. I push the head of my stick, edging him out, and the ball pops away from both of us. We scramble, but it's rolling fast, and I see Toby and Dion ready at the line, and I know they're both praying the ball makes it that far.

Percy gets to it first and kicks it to a waiting Toby, who scoops and runs. The way he cuts loose, I know Toby's not going to bother passing; he's headed straight for the goal.

I feel more than see the SB jersey streaking like a rocket across the field: Otto.

Like a charging bull, he's blind to anything but Toby, and my instincts tell me this time Otto isn't going for a trip. He wants to take Toby out.

I pick up speed. This is not a team loyalty thing, it's a right versus wrong thing, and *nobody* is going to mow down my best friend. Especially not Otto Penrod *the Third*.

I've got to get between them.

I put all I have into my run, spinning possible scenarios as I go. Within a yard of Toby I line up with Otto, somehow managing to skirt ahead of him by half a leg. There's only one way to do this. I use my body as a barricade and reach my stick out, bringing it down on Toby's before Otto can hit him. But Otto's killer momentum has to go somewhere, and there's no time to brace myself before his helmet and body come slamming into me. I drop to the turf, stunned, sticks swiping the ground around me to get to the loose ball.

I can't get up. And the next thing I know, play has stopped; was there a whistle?

Coach is standing over me, along with the SB trainer.

"Max, are you okay?"

Max? Who's Max? Then I remember. "Yeah, I think so."

They help me up and support me as I find my footing. I glance around at the players. They've all taken knees—except Otto. I ignore the accusing look he's sending me and turn to find Toby.

When we lock eyes, like we have a million times before, I wish I could say something. But he nods with the respect and sportsmanship Gramps drilled into us and puts his gloves together, starting the applause that follows me off the field.

Coach and the trainer are by my side, helping me, and as we cross the sideline, the head ref appears in front of us, his mouth set grimly. "He needs to be evaluated for a concussion before he can return to the field."

"That's exactly what we're going to do," says the trainer.

"There's something else, Coach," says the ref. "Number twenty-three is a live one out there. He should have been the one sitting out on that last penalty." Then he points to me. "Your player here just saved him from a definite three minutes—you get control of him or I will."

Coach takes a breath before answering. "I understand." He turns to the assistant coach. "Pull Otto and put Matt and Carlson in," he says. Then he gestures to me as the trainer leads me to the bench. "Let me know when he can play."

I hear a voice call my fake name and look to the stands. It's Amber. She mouths *Are you okay?* and I nod back at her. There are two suits walking down the steps beside her. One of them looks familiar, but I've seen so many suits lately it's hard to place him. They must be limo drivers, though, because they're both wearing those weird caps.

Just beyond them, on the other side of the stairs, sits our bus driver: Gran.

I quickly look back at Amber, and in my hurry to avoid Gran, who is probably worried about me dying from a head injury, my eyes accidentally flit to Laci—who is watching me.

Her eyes, even from twenty yards, hit me harder than Otto just did. I drop to the bench, my heart pounding.

Laci is the last person I want to think about right now.

## 24

I sit as my thoughts buzz from Laci, to the game in front of me, to Toby, to Otto, to Kyle, to the huge amount of security, to the odds that something might happen to Kyle at this game, and then to James, who's beside me on the bench.

"Are you okay?"

I look from the game, where Masters has possession, back to James. Maybe it's the hit to my head, but my brain feels fuzzy. Even if something is up with his family, there's no way I can keep tabs on James, too.

"I'm okay. Just waiting for the trainer." The sooner he checks me out, the faster I can get back on the field.

James keeps his eyes on the game and his voice low. "I'm not the only one who made a major-league enemy today."

He can only be talking about one person. I bend forward and find Otto, who's methodically pacing back and forth behind Coach, shaking his head in short angry bursts. The sky is still a crisp blue, but there's a furiously dark storm cloud clinging to that guy. I shrug. "Maybe so, but he didn't give me a choice."

I meet James's eyes, and he gives me a quick nod. "You woke me up today. I just want to say thanks."

Huh. He's acting like I saved him from getting creamed. "Sure."

The moment's way too serious, and we both know it. James stands and forces a laugh. "So what's your dad not cooking for dinner tonight?"

"Don't know, but I'll ask. Maybe you can come over—we can spy on your dorm room and see if anybody shows."

"Carrington!" the trainer calls as he heads toward the bench. "Let's take a look at you."

James slips back to the sidelines with the rest of the team, and I catch a glimpse of the board. The score is 2–2 with less than three minutes till the half.

The trainer puts a bag of ice on the bench, then tells me to stand still and balance on my right foot. After a series of tests, he says everything looks good but asks how I'm feeling. When I insist I'm fine, he says to be careful; if I get another knock on the head, I'm out for good.

I'm tempted to tell him I'm better off in the game, where Otto can't get to me.

Coach puts me on midfield at the start of the third quarter, and I even manage to get a point on the board. The teams are pretty evenly matched, and I have a few more opportunities to shoot, but I decide to pass for the assist instead. For some reason, that feels better. I want to play, but this game is about something else.

By the time it's over, Sydney Brown manages to beat Masters by two goals. If we meet each other again, it'll be in the play-offs.

I line up with the rest of the SB team, making sure to get between Kyle and James as we go through for the shake, and remember not to open my mouth. Not a single Masters player gives me a second look as we pass each other and grip hands. Toby's one of the last, and we actually lock eyes.

Nothing.

As the teams split off and head back to the benches, I'm relieved and bummed all at the same time. My team won, but I played against my team.

I have to let it go. It's over, and I gotta keep the focus on my job.

I locate Kang and make sure he's closing in on Kyle as the team gets their gear together and starts to head back to the bus. So far everybody's okay.

And then, like a noose, the circle begins to tighten fast. Kang and about ten suits are stepping around players between Kyle and them, eyes alert and hands ready to draw their weapons. This doesn't feel like business as usual. My heart is pumping fast, warning me to be ready—something is wrong.

I grab my bag and step closer to Kyle, and almost as an afterthought, I reach for James's shoulder and pull him next to me. Kang eyes James and me but makes no move to nudge us away from Kyle, the way the agents have with everybody else.

Kyle looks up, confused, as he grabs his gear and stands. There's a wall of suits blocking everything and everyone. "What's going on?" he says to Kang.

I let my eyes slowly circle the agents and try to see beyond them. Are they reacting to something?

"There's word of a specific threat, sir. We need to transport you now."

Kyle's eyes snap wide open, angry. "There's always a threat. Are you kidding?"

Kang doesn't want to take the time to explain. He bends down so he and Kyle are nose to nose; he's within an inch of pushing the first kid forward. "No, sir. We need to move quickly. A car is waiting."

James and I are looking back and forth between Kyle and Kang and each other, not sure what to do.

Kyle glares up at the agent. "Nothing ever happens. I'm going on the bus."

"I'll have to clear it, and you know how long that will take."

Kyle groans. "Please, Agent Kang. This was a big game."

Kang hesitates for a moment and then stands upright, presses his earpiece and grunts into his lapel. It's easy to see that the whole thing will be a huge pain, but it also seems like he understands.

After a few seconds he turns back to Kyle. "We need five minutes to reposition."

"Really?" Kyle says, grinning. "Thanks, Agent Kang. I owe you one."

Kang's lips turn up into what might almost be an answering smile, but quickly realize their mistake and return to the usual straight-line position. He nods and takes two steps back, eyeing the field around us.

"You guys don't have to wait," Kyle says to me and James.

"It's okay," I say. "I like how you roll, with the escort and all."

James agrees with a nod as he surveys all the firepower within fifteen feet of us. "Yeah, I don't mind waiting."

A few minutes more than Kang promised, the three of us are moving across the field inside an ovalish wall of black suits, and I'm feeling my real school's turf beneath me every step of the way. Ahead of the suits, I catch a glimpse of my Masters teammates entering the locker room. SB isn't a bad school, and I like most of my new teammates, but I'm fighting a strong urge to head over there and be with the guys who just lost an important game. Masters is home, and those guys are my brothers—brothers who would understand, if only I could tell them why I'm here.

I shake off the sorry-for-myself feeling as we climb aboard the bus. There are more Suburbans and official sedans than there were on the trip over, which is saying something.

The bus ride home is usually good when a team wins, but with the security delay and the five suits plus Kang—and Gran—it's not exactly relaxed. Kyle's presence makes a regular drive home complicated. Add a "threat," and right now it's a three-ring circus.

Otto is keeping to himself in the seat behind Bus Driver Gran, not talking to anybody. I don't think he's ever been taken out of a game like that before, and it's difficult to tell if he's still mad or has moved on to moping. He hasn't had a great afternoon, that's for sure.

Kyle leans over his seat and sticks his head between me and James. He's pretty aggravated, too. "Did you see how many agents were at the game?" he says, gesturing to Kang and a couple of other suits, a few rows back.

Both James and I turn to look.

"He said there was a threat, right?" I say.

"Don't worry," Kyle says, rolling his eyes. "Stuff never happens."

"You never know, Kyle," I say. "I'd take it a little more seriously if I were you."

Kyle laughs and leans down between James and me. "Why should I when I've got all of them taking it seriously for me?" Then he straightens up again with a long groan. "It's ridiculous. This is how they overreact to every single 'threat.' What do they think, the North Koreans are going to send a military squad over to get me?" He lets out a long breath. "I'll be living behind a wall of black suits till the end of high school, just because of my dad's job. Think about it," he says, making a quick circle motion with his finger at all the agents within spitting distance. "Would you want to deal with *them* all the time?"

James is quiet, like he's actually giving the question thought. He faces front again, and I'm not sure if he's answering Kyle or not, because it's barely a whisper; but I hear him. "Maybe. If it would keep trouble away."

I don't know what to say to Kyle or James, so I look out the bus window. It's still light outside, but not for long.

I'm understanding Kyle a lot better now. He's caught up in a life he never chose, and he's stuck. Sort of like a prisoner, but with better food and a much more comfortable bed. And not only does he need protection from bad-guy adults, he needs protection from kids like Otto, too.

James is different. I know Gran said he's probably nervous because of whatever's going on with his family, but his dad has to be pretty rotten for his mom and him to go through all this to make a new life. And what he just said is top-of-the-Richter-scale strange. It's time to get to the bottom of what's really going on with him.

I poke James's arm. I haven't asked, but I'm betting Gran or Captain Thompson won't mind. "So you want to come to my house for dinner? I'm pretty sure my dad can keep trouble away, at least for a couple of hours."

James laughs. "If he can do that, I'm moving in."

I don't think he's joking.

## wednesday, may 9, 7:50 p.m.

# 25

Captain Thompson has the phone to his ear when he walks into the cover house.

He spots James and me at the kitchen table doing homework and immediately pulls a postcard out of his jacket pocket and hands it to me. My mouth begins to water at the picture on the front. It's an ad for a local pizza place that delivers.

"Dad" takes the phone from his ear and holds it against his chest. "Call them and get two large pies and some side salads," he says before heading down the hall toward his bedroom. "Let me know when it gets here. I've got work to do."

I pick up my phone and can't dial fast enough. It's been forever since I bit into a fresh slice of pizza. In other words: four whole days.

"Is your housekeeper off for the night?"

I stare back at James. It takes me a second before I understand what he's asking. I'm pretty sure I can't explain that our housekeeper is really my grandmother and that she's probably in the back of some blacked-out Suburban peeling off her bus driver face, hair and duds and finding out what the heck happened near the field tonight, before she can show up here and put an apron on.

I shake my head. "She'll probably be here soon."

I order the pizza and then notice I have a couple of texts. The first one is from Toby.

**We lost to SB by 2. Might c them in play-offs. Hope ur back.**

The second one is from Kyle; we exchanged numbers at lunch today.

**O is nuts mad. Asked for J rm #**

I show it to James, who gives me an uneasy look. "What do you think he'll do? And when?"

"He probably wants to find some dirt on you, same as everyone else. But who knows when?" Then I see what James is worried about. "He won't break into your room if he thinks you're there. If I had to guess, I'd say he'll try tomorrow morning sometime, when everybody's down at the school."

"Can we check the cameras?"

I hesitate, realizing I'm going to have to cross the Special Service wall in my phone in front of James. I hold it so he can't see what I'm doing. "Sure," I say as I press the screen with my thumb and punch the passwords.

It takes less than a minute to pull up the views from both cameras. The room is empty, as it should be. I lean over and show James.

He grins as he examines both angles. "Cool," he says. "Is this live?"

"Yep," I say. "And it's recorded, so we can go back in time if we need to. Not only that, I set it so I get a notification if there's movement in the room."

"The cameras have motion detectors?" James narrows

his eyes at me. "So the app came with the cameras? Where'd you get this stuff?"

Uh-oh. "It's something my dad's company is working on. I don't think it's for sale yet."

James looks back to the screen. "You're right. Otto probably won't try anything until tomorrow."

I nudge James. "Why don't you make it easy on him and leave your door unlocked?"

He grins back at me, and I get another glimpse of the real James, the one who's in control of his life. "I like the way you think."

It's hard to know how to do it, but it's now or never, so I ask him point-blank. "Is your dad dangerous? Is that why you're hiding?"

James's mouth drops open and he shakes his head. "No." Then he turns and checks the back hall to make sure we're alone. When he looks at me again, he lowers his voice. "I don't really know all of it. Even if I did, I couldn't say anything. Anyway, the whole thing will be over next week. My mom is coming to get me and we're leaving DC."

What? "You're moving again? Why?"

James frowns. "Simple. If we don't move and start over somewhere else, she'll never be safe. And neither will I."

Pins and needles prickle my spine. This doesn't sound good.

"I'm confused. Is your dad that bad?"

James sits up in his chair, immediately defensive. "Why do you keep asking about my dad?"

Um. Not sure what to say to that. "I just thought you were hiding from him."

James shakes his head. "No. It's complicated. *Really* complicated. My mom double-crossed the wrong people. That's why I'm lying low at SB. My mom thought that with all the bodyguards and security I'd be safe while she's making everything right again." James presses his pencil into his book; he draws a quick circle and then starts filling it in, dark and hard. "Every time I see somebody strange at the school, I panic. I guess I'm just being paranoid."

"You mean about them finding you?"

James sighs. He lets his pencil drop and looks up at me. "Yeah. And I'm worried about my mom. What she's doing—it's dangerous."

"Where exactly is your mom, James?"

He pushes his chair back and stands and walks over to the window. At first I'm not sure what he's looking at, and then I realize there's a reason he's facing the closed blinds. His shoulders begin to tremble and he puts his head in his hands. Between careful breaths, he whispers, "I—don't—know."

I cross the room and stand behind him. I'm not sure what else to do, so I put my hand on his shoulder and wait. After a couple of breaths he turns. His face is red and blotchy. "Sorry," he says in a weak voice.

The sound of the front door opening sends us scrambling back to the table. We plop in our seats and start flipping notebook pages as Gran, aka our housekeeper, rounds the corner and enters the kitchen. She briefly looks us over before heading toward the counter, where she plunks down two grocery bags. "I understand pizza will be here soon. Would you boys like salad?"

"Don't worry," I say. "Dad's on top of things. He told us to order salad, too."

And with that, we all go back to pretending everything is normal.

But it's definitely not.

After James is gone and I'm getting ready for bed, Gran and Captain Dad appear in my doorway.

"We thought we should let you know about the report we just received. Ever since the false alarm about the game tonight, all evidence of any online activity has been removed; the messages and posts mentioning SB were deleted; it's all gone dead," says the captain. Then he turns to Gran. "Are you going to tell him the rest, or should I?"

I sit on the edge of my bed. "Our job is over? Done?"

Gran chuckles. "No. However, you may receive a promotion."

I cock my head. "What do you mean?"

"The detail I have working on the cable repairman's investigation finally made it to his home. They found a briefcase full of cash—a good deal of cash—under his bed. Apparently his wife was shocked to see it, especially in light of all their unpaid bills. She also says he's been acting strange over the past week or so." Gran pauses a moment before continuing. "There's evidence he's connected to the hack job, stealing Sydney Brown computer records. We're holding him for continued questioning, and there will be a full investigation."

Captain Thompson walks across the room and puts out his hand. "A little late saying so, but nicely done, Clayton. We're in the process of tracking the money, and we've ordered satellite surveillance records on his normal routes for the past sixty days. It will take work, but we'll figure it out."

I accept the captain's hand and shake. He's smiling like a proud dad, and I grin right back at him.

Gran moves beside the captain. She's still looking a little dazed, like she's having trouble understanding the news. "Normally, data breaches originate overseas, but it's looking as if this attack was politically motivated. Someone local is trying to find specific information about parents of Sydney Brown students. It could be connected to the next election or something similar."

"So Kyle isn't in danger?"

When Captain Thompson answers, he says each word slowly and deliberately. "It doesn't appear so."

Gran leans down and pats my shoulder. "We'll alert Kang and his detail, and the president, of course. For now, the critical threat seems to have passed. We'll keep you at Sydney Brown through the end of the school year to make sure, but I suspect the worst is behind us."

After they leave, I fall asleep in the bed that's not my bed thinking about Gran's words.

Is it possible that this is almost over?

# 26

Thursday morning comes fast, and before I know it I'm at school, throwing an empty coffee cup in the garbage and heading to Advanced World History. There's lacrosse practice this afternoon to get ready for play-offs, and it can't come soon enough.

Now that I don't have to worry about going against my Masters buds, or about whoever is behind the computer hacking and Internet posts Gran and the captain have been so crazy about, or about making friends with Kyle, lacrosse practice is back to number one fun.

I'm about to turn the corner when I hear familiar voices and immediately put the brakes on. There's no mistaking Otto's voice. Which reminds me of the one thing I don't want to deal with today. But I have to. Taking care of that kid is the only way Kyle is going to return to "himself" and maybe get his friendship with Amber back on the right track. Something both of them need, whether they admit it or not.

"So you're with me. You'll help me convince Peter it's time to drop out? I'm ready. The debate's after lunch."

Kyle reassures him, telling him the story we came up with. "I already talked to him. He's tired of the whole election anyway."

"Good. One bird down. Now it's time to get even with that James kid—show him he can't mess with us."

"What are you going to do?" Kyle deserves one of those big gold acting awards. The sincerity in his voice is unbelievable—in a believable way.

The bell is about to ring, so I get moving. Besides, I want to see his face when Otto actually answers that question. I take the corner at a wide angle, in time to catch Otto smirking and leaning into Kyle. "Search and seizure, my friend. Search and seizure."

Kyle catches my eye as I walk past. "Hey, Max. Good game last night."

"Thanks," I say, deliberately ignoring Otto. "You, too." My favorite Advanced World History class is waiting, so I keep moving.

A couple of minutes later Kyle lands in the desk beside me. He's texting.

I feel a regular vibration on my phone and tap the screen.

**Heads up. Next period is his free 1.**

I don't look at Kyle. I don't need to. I send him back a happy face.

Forty-eight minutes later, Amber is waiting for me outside World History. "The debate is at twelve thirty, right after lunch. What do you think? Who'll show up, Otto or Peter?"

I hold up my SpiPhone. "May the best man show," I say.

Amber grins as she turns and heads to her second-period class. "Keep me posted."

Kyle knocks me in the arm from behind. I cock my head his way, but he's watching Amber walk down the hall. "Girls are such pains," he says.

I laugh. "Yeah, especially that one."

Kyle grunts something incomprehensible, then gestures to my phone. "I'd bet money Otto is halfway to the dorm by now. Remember, when you have video, send it to me and James—and Amber, I guess. Then we corner him as soon as he gets back."

I nod. "Not that I usually pay attention in math, but I think it's gonna be worse today."

"Don't let Ms. Miller catch you with that phone during class. She's getting super-strict."

He's right about that; she took three yesterday. I tuck it in my pocket and wonder how many times I can go to the bathroom in forty-eight minutes. I sit at my desk and pull it back out for one last look at the video feed from James's room.

I almost jump out of my seat. How can Otto be there already?

I look closer, enlarging the feed so I can see better.

No. No. No.

My heart is skipping beats as I lean across the aisle and whisper. "Kyle, I don't know if this is going to work."

Kyle narrows his eyes. "What do you mean?"

"Because I think Otto sent his driver to do his dirty work."

"What?" Kyle shakes his head. "That doesn't make any sense."

The bell rings and there's a last-minute race for seats. I don't know what to do. Video of some man whose face is hidden by his chauffeur cap won't do us any good against Otto. He'll laugh in our faces.

We need real proof: evidence that whoever it is in James's dorm room now is helping Otto. And there's only one way to get that.

As the real Algebra I students get settled, I give a thumbs-up to Kyle. Then I hold my breath and twist my face into as pitiful a look as I can manage and raise my hand.

"Yes, Max?" calls Ms. Miller from her desk.

By now I must be almost blue. I slowly let the air out of my nose and murmur, "I'm not feeling well," as I put my hand to my head and let it drop halfway to the desk.

Ms. Miller is by my side in an instant. She pulls me up and starts to slowly walk me to the door. "You need to get to the nurse's office. We had several students out with the flu two weeks ago. We don't want a repeat of that."

I give her a weak nod. "I probably just need to lie down for a few minutes."

"You're very flushed," she says, her brow creased in concern as we enter the hallway. "Don't come back unless you're really feeling better. Do you know where the clinic is? I can have one of the students accompany you."

I have no idea where the clinic is, but since that's not where I'm going, it doesn't matter. "No, I can get there on my own. Thanks, Ms. Miller."

I teeter down the hall until I hear the math room door shut. With a quick check on Kang and one of his men, posted at opposite ends of the hall, I start to accelerate.

Once I turn the corner, I run like heck to the next stair-well and take the steps to the lower level two at a time. I burst out the exit door into blinding sunlight, which hits me like a brick wall. I stop and look both ways, shielding my eyes with my hand.

I know for a fact kids run between the dorm and school when they forget something, even though it's supposed to be against school rules, so I'm not worried anybody's gonna stop me. On the other hand—I look way up the long hill to where the roofline of the dorms pops out of the trees—it's a long haul.

For a split second I think about borrowing one of the golf carts parked outside the boys' locker room. But getting caught in one of the precious SB golf carts again might turn the odds 100 percent against me. Not smart to chance it.

I squint and take off into the morning light, pushing my legs as fast as they'll go. In seconds I'm at the line of trees that stretch along the school's south perimeter, all the way to the dorms. It's almost too quiet as I run.

I slow my pace as I approach the dorm, and crouch down on the sidewalk, between the familiar lines of box-wood shrubs and golf carts. I take a long look around. Where is Otto? He's got to be somewhere around here.

I take another few steps and then slip between the golf carts. They're getting to be my favorite hiding spot. As I peek from behind the plastic bench seats, I notice a limo waiting at the end of the canopied entrance. Figures. Otto's such a jerk, hiding in the limo, getting somebody else to do this for him.

I need him to show himself. I've at least got to get a shot of the license plate, to prove he's connected to all this.

I get my SpiPhone out and make double sure the camera's ready to catch whatever happens. I'm tempted to flip to the other app, the one that's hooked up to James's dorm room, but then I might miss the driver when he leaves. I can't make a mistake this time.

I don't have to wait long. The door cracks open, and I hold my cell phone up, making sure the screen catches the whole entrance area, and tap Record.

The same cap-wearing guy I saw in James's dorm room pokes his head out and takes a look around before he opens the door all the way. Then he shoves through, holding a large box with a computer monitor sticking out of it. Right behind him, another guy in an identical driver's uniform is following—with Otto.

This is awesome. We've got him!

I keep recording, checking my screen to make sure I'm really actually definitely recording. My heart is racing now, this time with excitement. I watch the first man put the box in the trunk as the second man opens the rear door of the limo for Otto and then gets in behind him. Man #1 walks around the car and gets into the driver's seat.

Three elevated heartbeats later, the engine comes to life and the limo takes off around the circle and speeds down the drive.

I look at my screen and hit Replay. If Otto weren't so downright despicable, I'd leap across the golf carts in joy. The second time through, the scene is even more mind-blowing. Otto Penrod *the Third* has a hard drive's worth of nerve. Did he seriously take James's computer?

I stand and turn toward the school. Between the tape of Otto and his dudes stealing James's computer, and whatever else happened in that dorm room, we've got him good. No way he can push Peter out of the election or bully any of the SB kids again.

Not only that, I'm beginning to feel a lot better, too. I predict a miraculous recovery by the time I get back to math class. Ms. Miller is going to be very pleased.

# 27

I make it to algebra with eight minutes left in the class. Ms. Miller eyes me as I enter the room. "Are you sure you should be here, Max?"

I walk down the aisle, hoping she doesn't decide to examine me. I ran hard, and I can feel a bead of sweat trickle down my cheek. If she sees it, she might go into a panic and take me to the nurse herself. I quickly wipe my face with my shirtsleeve, then turn as I sit. "Yes, ma'am. I'm okay now."

She raises her eyebrows and then points behind her desk. "The assignment is on the board. What you don't finish is homework."

Nobody except Kyle is paying attention to me; they're busy being brilliant SB students, solving the assigned problems. For a split second I wonder what that kind of brilliance is like, until Kyle leans across the aisle and brings me back to reality. "Well?"

I sneak a glance his way as I copy what's on the board—for later—and whisper out of the side of my mouth. "I think we're good, but I haven't looked at the room feed yet. Time to text Otto. Tell him you need to talk to him about the debate."

Kyle nods. "Okay. What about James and Amber?"

"You and I should confront Otto face-to-face. I don't trust him, and the fewer people involved, the better."

For the final minutes, I sit at the desk with my pencil stuck to one single point on my notebook. It's not even 10 a.m., and it feels like a whole day's gone by already. I need to shake myself awake. Maybe a donut, or another mocha.

I put my pencil down and edge the SpiPhone out of my pocket. The second hand on the wall clock directly above Ms. Miller's head is ticking its way around—less than a minute before the bell rings.

I cast an eye to the dark screen and bring it to life. I can at least check my texts, and maybe get a message started to James and Amber.

Ms. Miller appears from out of nowhere, hand out, palm up. "That's the third time I've seen you look at your phone, Max, and you haven't even spent ten minutes with us this period."

Seriously? She can't have my phone. I need it. "But I—" There's no finishing that sentence. What am I going to tell her, after I already got away with skipping most of her class? I place the phone in her hand.

"You may have it after lunch," she says on her way up the aisle. Then she opens her desk drawer and drops my phone inside.

The bell rings, and I grab my stuff.

"I warned you," says Kyle, falling in with me as we make our escape.

"Yeah, I know," I say, wanting to kick myself. "Did you hear from Otto?"

He takes his phone out of his pocket and stares at the screen, shaking his head. "Nothing," he says. "Did you actually see him up there?"

I nod, then gesture to Ms. Miller as we pass her on the way out of the room. "But it's all on my phone."

"What happened?"

"Long story," I say. "Let's go find Amber and James. I'll tell you all at the same time."

We scramble down the hall together with an immediate triangle of bodyguards in our wake. I look over my shoulder at Kang as we jog, and then at Kyle, who rolls his eyes back at me.

"Gets old, doesn't it?" he says.

He's POTUS's only son. Yeah, it gets old, but it's so *he* gets old.

Amber is pacing outside English, obviously waiting for us. When she sees us appear around the corner, she waves her hands in the air and runs in our direction, meeting us halfway. She hooks her arms into Kyle's and mine and pulls us to the nearest alcove. "What happened?"

"There's good news, and there's bad news."

Amber gives a little *hrmphh*. "When Otto is involved, everything is bad news."

Okay, that might be true. "Have you seen James?"

Amber pulls on my shirtsleeve. "No, but the bell's about to ring. Spill."

Kyle is waiting, too. I take a deep breath, and it all comes out. "Math was getting ready to start, and I looked at my phone. There was a limo driver in James's room, and I figured Otto sent him. Since we need to have something on Otto, not his driver, I got out of class and went to the dorms to figure out what was going on. The limo was parked outside, so I waited. And then the driver came out with a big box of stuff, including James's computer. But that's not all. Otto was right behind him, with another driver. Or maybe his bodyguard."

Kyle nods. "He's got security. Not like me, but he does. And I know he makes them do all sorts of crud, like get him burritos. Who knows what Otto told them? Maybe he said he bought the computer from James."

Amber frowns. "Is that the good news, or the bad news?"

"The good news is that I saw it happen and got it on video. And we have whatever happened in James's room recorded, too."

"And the bad news?"

"Uh, Ms. Miller took my phone and won't give it back till after lunch, so we don't have anything to hold over Otto's head."

Amber shakes her head. "We have enough. You just have to bluff when you talk to him. And he can smell weakness a mile away, so whatever you do, be confident. He's got to believe you'll make the whole thing public, because that won't embarrass just him, but his dad, too. And his dad is a monster when he gets mad. I almost feel sorry for Otto sometimes."

"I think you're right, Amber." Then I turn to Kyle. "Did you talk to Peter? What's he say about the debate?"

"After I told him what Otto has been doing to kids, he

said he'd do it. But I'm worried. Talk about embarrassed, this buying votes thing going around about his dad really got to him, especially since it's not true."

Amber nods sympathetically. "Of course it did. But he's the right person to represent the Stripes."

Back to the point of all this. "Nothing from Otto?"

Kyle looks at his phone. "Huh. Nothing. That's strange. Usually I have like twenty texts from him by third period."

At the sound of the bell, we head into English together. "He's too busy conquering the world. He can't answer texts," I say as we walk through the doorway.

Suddenly, Amber stops and pivots to face us. "James doesn't know about this?"

I shake my head. "Nope. We need to tell him."

"I sure don't want to see his face when he finds out about his computer," says Amber. "Do you guys have any classes with him?"

"I usually don't see him much except at lacrosse, and next period, in art," I say. "I know for a fact he's going crazy thinking about all this, though. And we need to find Otto, too. I don't know what he's planning to do to James, but it has to be serious if he's going to all this trouble."

"Yeah, James could probably use one of Kyle's body-guards," says Amber.

Even if she's joking, she's sort of right.

The three of us look at each other. What do we do? Going to actual classes is beginning to get in the way of our plan. "Do you think Mr. Tatum would give us another pass?"

A deep, gargly throat-clearing noise clues us in to Mr. Tatum's presence. He inserts his head between ours.

"I think *Mr. Tatum* has not seen enough of you three this week. And Romeo and Juliet have gotten themselves into a predicament that you won't want to miss." He steps back and extends his arm toward the classroom. "Please join us."

As we cross the room to our seats, something way down in my gut is telling me, Romeo and Juliet aren't the only ones heading into a predicament.

## 28

I have no idea what's going on with Shakespeare's most famous couple, Romeo and Juliet. None. And I'm pretty sure Kyle and Amber don't, either. All through English we've been slipping each other notes the old-fashioned way, on paper, since I'm phoneless.

We've decided that Amber will find Peter and Monique to make sure they're ready for the debate, while Kyle and I break the news to James that he's down a computer. On the upside, once we confront Otto about his crime, SB might be down a bully—and a thief.

If we can find him, that is. Kyle still hasn't heard anything. And nobody's seen him.

At the sound of the bell, we practically fly to art class. Kang must have gotten the word about the big Kyle alert going down a notch, because it's only him and another agent, and they're staying more than twenty feet back.

We check the classroom, but James hasn't arrived yet. Kyle taps me on the shoulder. "Can you put my stuff on the table? I'm going to look for Otto. I think he has science now, and it's right down the hall."

I get my rolled-up piece of "art" and grab Kyle's, too. Besides containers of pencils and tinted charcoals and markers, Mr. Walsh keeps a huge basket of rocks on each table so we can keep our drawings flat. I unroll mine and place a rock at each corner.

I decide to do the same for Kyle; I grab a few more rocks and spread out his paper. His scene has come along. There's no mistaking Kyle's self-portrait as he stands front and center between two crowds of people tugging him by each arm. There are kids waving political signs and bodyguards with their guns out, and reporters with cameras flashing. There's a huge explosion in the background, which has launched both an elephant and a donkey into the air.

Not exactly subtle, but if I were Mr. Walsh, I'd give him an A-plus.

"That's pretty good," says James over my shoulder.

"It's Kyle's," I say, turning to him. I know he doesn't really want to talk about art.

"What's happened? Did he do anything yet?" James looks down at my pocket. "Show me already!"

"Ms. Miller took my phone, so I can't show you this exact second, but we have him on video—I think."

James's eyes bug out. "What do you mean, *you think*?"

"Don't worry, we have the most important part. I just never got the chance to look at the feed, so I don't know exactly what happened in your room—whether it was Otto or his driver who took your computer."

"My computer?" James's chin recedes and he cranks his eyebrows forward. "Why the heck would he take that?"

Mr. Walsh claps his hands for everybody to sit and get to work just as Kyle comes skidding into the room and swerves into his chair. Kyle looks up at us. "He's not there."

James drops into his seat. "Would one of you tell me what's going on?"

I sit between them, baffled. "How can Otto not show up to science class? Where could he be?"

"Knowing him, he's deconstructing the computer to sell it for parts on eBay," says Kyle with a short chuckle. Then he goes straight-faced. "I'm kidding. He's probably getting what he needs before he sends his driver back with it, like the whole thing never happened."

Oh, that's brilliant. And exactly what Otto would do.

"Won't he get in trouble for skipping?"

"Otto?" This time Kyle's laugh sounds real. "They're so tired of dealing with him and his father, teachers don't even bother anymore. He's been telling me I would get away with a ton more stuff if I tried, but to be honest, I don't mind school."

I turn to James, who's bent over his dead-man-in-car-falling-in-the-ocean, frantically shading a crate of over-flowing fish. "Are you okay?"

"I can't believe he stole my computer. My dad gave it to me the last time I saw him—he said I needed a desktop for my art." He shakes his head. "Man, I can't wait to get out of here."

I lower my voice. "Did you hear from your mom?"

James picks up a piece of sand-colored charcoal and begins to work on the woman in the window. "Not yet. But I think she's finished testifying at the end of next week." He stops coloring and stares at Kyle and me. "Is one of you going to tell me what happened this morning?"

Kyle and I exchange glances. "Go for it," he says to me.

I turn back to James. "It all started when I checked the camera feed from your place," I start. And in a lower-than-low voice, I fill him in on every single detail.

Heading to the cafeteria, I realize it's my fourth lunch at Sydney Brown, but it's the first time I've walked there with friends. I'm about to follow Kyle and James through the cafeteria doors when a sudden splash of liquid soaks my pants.

"I'm so sorry, young man," says a familiar-looking member of the janitorial staff. "Let me help you get cleaned up."

Uh-oh. I quickly glance ahead at Kyle, who's holding the door open. Both he and James are waiting awkwardly, not sure where to look: me, my wet pants or the janitor lady. "Um, I'll catch up with you guys in a minute," I say.

James nods, and I watch as Kyle lets go of the door and they both head inside the cafeteria. Then I catch up with my grandmother, who's moved to a quiet place farther down the hallway.

She takes out a towel as I approach and bends to pat my leg dry. "I've sent three texts and called twice. I was beginning to think you must be handcuffed and hanging from a rooftop somewhere." She looks up and raises one eyebrow accusingly. "That is obviously not the case."

"The math teacher took my phone," I say. Something's off; I can feel it. She wouldn't be here if there weren't a problem. "What's wrong?"

Her lips form a thin, tight line before she answers. "We have news, but I don't want you to worry."

Conversations that start out this way, especially when

it's my grandmother talking, are never good. I have an immediate flashback to when she told me Gramps was missing. Three days later, the "I don't want you to worry" turned into another conversation. He'd been found, dead, on the banks of the Potomac River.

I stare down at her, my heart pumping fast. I want to ask what happened, and who it happened to, but I'm afraid. I force the question out of my mouth. "Is it Captain Thompson?"

"No, Derek is fine," she says. "But Carlos is in the hospital. He was ambushed and shot three times as he was shielding the witness he's been transporting. Thank goodness he was wearing his vest." She gives her head a quick shake. "They've used decoy vehicles with a multitude of convoys, and four different safe houses—and Carlos varied the routes each time they traveled. They've done everything they could to muddy the waters, but this crime syndicate has still managed to find them—they mean business."

This witness must be super-important to need all that protection. What did he see, a murder? "Carlos and his witness—they're okay?"

Gran stands. "Carlos is doing fine, considering, and so far, the witness is safe," she whispers. "But I'll be hard to reach for the rest of the day because Derek and I will be helping the marshals. Tomorrow is an important day for the case, and with Carlos recovering, they need our support—and a new tactical driver. It will be difficult to replace him."

I haven't seen Carlos for weeks. Right after the mall napper case, he made me my favorite cake for my thirteenth birthday. It was huge, a four-level sponge cake with custard filling and berries and whipped cream. He put a huge pickle on top, too, just to be funny. I hate pickles, but I love Carlos.

Gran's wrong. Forget difficult, it would be impossible to replace Carlos. "Did you see him? He's really okay?"

She nods. "You can visit him this weekend, but the doctors say he'll recover quickly." She pauses and glances quickly at the empty halls around us. "I think things are secure around here for the moment. I did speak with the president, and he's agreed that while he's in school, Kyle doesn't need as much close security."

"That's good. I think that will help."

Gran narrows her eyes. "It's good until there's a problem. The pressure is on you now."

I want to tell her not to worry, but she keeps talking. "I'm only here to let you know about Carlos, and that Derek and I will see you at home tonight." Then she steps back and raises her voice. "I'm so sorry for ruining your pants, young man. I'm more than happy to wash them if you'll give them to me."

I guess our undercover meeting is over.

"Uh, it's okay. My housekeeper will take care of them when I get home."

The corner of Gran's mouth quakes in a brief but amused smirk before she picks up her towel and starts to walk away. "A boy your age doesn't do his own laundry?"

"She won't let me," I say, feeling a grin stretch across my face.

"I should speak with her about that," she clucks over her shoulder.

And before I can come back with a good response, she's gone.

## 29

I enter the cafeteria and immediately see three sets of arms waving me to a table in the back. I'm hungry, so for half a second I think about getting food first, but I decide to see what's so important that Kyle, James and Amber are all acting like cheerleaders doing a pom-pom routine.

When I get closer, I begin to cheer, too. On the inside.

There are two large Domino's pizza boxes sitting in the middle of the table. "Sometimes Kang orders out for me," explains Kyle, opening one of the boxes. "Help yourself."

He doesn't have to ask twice. I slide into the empty spot beside Amber and lift a slice to my mouth. I look around as I chew and swallow the first bite. "So where are your shadows?"

Kyle points to each of the exit doors. Sure enough, there's a suit posted at each one. "After last night's false alarm, which was probably the millionth one this year, I had it out with my dad. He said he couldn't remove the security, but he would check to see if they could back off. Kang must have gotten word sometime this morning." Kyle smiles as he adds, "It's weird. For the first time ever, my dad was actually cool about it."

For a second I wonder if the president was "cool" because I'm here. But then I remember: even though Kyle is safe, we've still got problems. "So what's going on with Peter? Is he ready for the debate?"

Amber shrugs. "As long as Otto doesn't show up at the last minute and try to take the podium."

I look at Kyle. "You still haven't heard from him? What do you think he's up to?"

Kyle shakes his head. "No idea. Maybe writing a speech or prepping for the debate? Last I heard, according to him, *he* was going to be the one debating Monique."

This election is the most important thing to Otto right now; I don't think he'll back down unless we force him.

I finish my first slice and pick up a second. As I bite into it, I glance at the clock on the far wall. It's 12:10—twenty minutes before the debate is supposed to begin.

James shuts the empty pizza box and picks it up as he stands. "I've got to go up to the dorms and get my backup stick so I have it for practice. I meant to bring it this morning, 'cause I'm having problems with my mesh." He salutes as he walks toward the door that leads outside. "See you guys at the debate."

I swing my legs over the bench and get up. "I'm going to Ms. Miller's room to get my phone."

Kyle stands up, too. "I'll come with you," he says. He pushes the last of the pizza toward Amber. There are three slices left, and he winks at her. "Eat up, Amber. You'll need your strength to report on the debate."

"Very funny," she says, closing the box. "I have to get going, too. I want a front-row seat. What do I do if Otto shows up?"

"Hold on, I just got a text." Kyle looks down at his phone. After a second he looks back at us, mouth open. "It's Otto." Kyle's eyes are flitting back and forth between us.

"What's wrong?" says Amber.

"He needs a ride," Kyle says. "But—he wants me to go to the locker room first and bring him his lacrosse stuff."

"Ride? Why would he need a ride?" says Amber.

Yeah, that doesn't make a lot of sense. "Or his lacrosse stuff?" I reach my hand out. "Can I see?"

**I'm stuck at Exxon. Need my practice uniform. Can u?**

"The Exxon at the bottom of the hill?" I say. "Why doesn't he walk?"

Kyle shrugs. "That's Otto. He probably expects me to send a car."

"This couldn't be more perfect," I say as I think it through. "I'll go with you, and we'll have our chat. We have time, 'cause technically we don't have to be at the debate." Then I chuckle. "And we can definitely make sure Otto misses it."

Amber stands and gets between us. "C'mon, you guys. The debate is important. It will help you decide who to vote for."

Kyle and I stare hard at Amber. Finally she shrinks a little. "All right, do what you need to do. But try to get back, okay?"

We nod at her, head out the rear door and take the back way around the school.

The locker room is empty, and for some reason I have a weird feeling about it. As Kyle spins the combination on Otto's locker, I realize why.

"Your security didn't come with us. Not even Kang."

Kyle freezes. "Are you kidding? Nobody?" He turns

slowly and scans the area around us. Nothing; not a soul, a suit or a sound.

"I didn't mean to lose them, but this is kind of cool. I feel free." A mischievous grin spreads across his face as he pulls out his phone and pushes the power button. "They track me with this thing, you know."

Yeah, I know. "I don't think you need to do that, Kyle."

"Maybe, but turning my phone off makes it feel like a real vacation. Anything could happen."

He's right about that. Instantly, Gran's words come back to me: *The pressure is on you now.*

"Uh, Kyle. Maybe we *should* send your driver with these," I say, pointing to the stack of clothes in his hands.

"Not a chance," he says. "Remember? We need to have a serious talk with Otto, and now's the perfect time. Let's go."

I take a deep breath and follow him out the door, right past the line of golf carts. I put on the brakes and clear my throat. "You know, if you want to make Amber happy, we might want to get back for the debate."

Kyle lifts an eyebrow. "Not that I want to make Amber happy, but Peter *is* my candidate," he says. "I should at least try to make it."

"Exactly." I ease toward the nearest cart, grab the SB maintenance cap resting on the steering wheel and offer it to Kyle. "It'd be silly not to speed up the process if we can."

Kyle jogs to the passenger side of the cart and puts the cap on his head as I slip behind the wheel. "I agree," he says, pointing to our left. "Take that path over there. There's a shortcut through the woods that ends at the back end of the gas station. It's a little rough, but we'll be there in three minutes, tops."

I glance at him and wonder how many ways this could go wrong. "Pull that brim down. I don't want anybody to know I've kidnapped the president's son."

We roll through the woods laughing and joking, ignoring any guilty thoughts about leaving school grounds, and Kyle's security, behind.

Sure enough, when we reach the bottom of the long, winding hill, we find the gas station parking lot. And idling right on the far corner of the roughly paved asphalt is the same black limousine from this morning: Otto's.

I turn to Kyle. "I still don't get it. Why would he need his practice gear? And why can't his driver take him back to school?"

Kyle shrugs. "All I know is, after we tell him what we've got on him, I'm done. No more jumping through his hoops. And nobody else will have to, either."

I turn off the golf cart and we walk over to the limo. The door pops open, and I watch Kyle stick his head inside.

His head snaps back to me. "Max," he says. "This was not such a good idea."

I bend down to look around him, but it's too dark to see anything.

A deep voice comes from the shadows. "You boys get in," it says in a thick accent. "We need to talk."

A shiver runs through me, and for a moment I can't move. Talk? Yeah, we want to talk, but probably not with somebody who sounds so intimidating.

My eyes dart around the parking lot, but the brutish

voice is quick to warn me. "Not a good idea to run, kid. Your friend here will pay for it if you do."

Kyle hunches over like he's going to hurl on the blacktop. I feel the same way. What the heck is going on?

I put my hand on Kyle's back and give him an *It's going to be okay* squeeze as we step inside. Not that I believe it. There are too many weapons I don't have for it to be okay: a sedative stick, a stun pen, a borrowed gun—not even my SpiPhone, thanks to Ms. Miller.

Kyle slides across the rear bench and I sit beside him and close my eyes, hoping to adjust to the darkness, and whatever that putrid stench is, a little faster. When I open them, I see the exact problem: a middle-aged man with a gun to Otto's neck.

The man knocks on the privacy glass. "Get moving," he tells the driver.

I am confused, so instead of doing the logical keep-my-mouth-shut thing, I talk. "Hey, Otto," I say, holding up his shooting shirt. "Brought your stuff. How's it going?"

Otto is a pale pinkish color and it's hard to tell, but I think he's shaking. I lean forward a little for a better look. From the rank smell and the condition of his bow tie and school shirt, he not only felt like throwing up, but actually did. I can understand why he needs a change of clothes.

Dang it. Somebody's got to figure this out, so I keep going. "I apologize for not helping you out this morning when I saw you. I thought these guys were your bodyguards. My bad."

Otto's eyes are widening, like he thinks I'm nuts.

"What's your name, kid?" The man's eyes are bulging and staring straight at me.

"I'm Max," I say. "I don't mean to rush things, but there's a very important debate going on at our school and they can't start without us, so—"

The man grins a beastly, jagged-toothed smile. "You can leave, no problem. We just need to find somebody." He jabs the gun farther into Otto's neck. "My men picked up the wrong kid this morning, and this young man can't seem to help us. He says you can, though."

Whoever these guys want is in big trouble. But one thing at a time. I turn to Kyle, who's just as pale as Otto. Which is saying something, since his skin is normally dark brown.

And then it occurs to me, do they know Kyle is *Kyle*? I was just joking around when I gave him the cap, but now I'm glad I did.

I'd better do all the talking. "Who are you looking for?" I'm praying a thousand prayers he doesn't say Kyle. The kid I'm supposed to be protecting. The same kid I basically escorted into this trap.

The man relaxes his arms, and his hands drop to his lap. Otto takes a deep breath, obviously relieved the gun is no longer an immediate threat.

"His name is Michael Basso," says the man. He hesitates for a second, and I replay the name in my mind, super-happy he didn't say Kyle—and that I've never heard of this Michael.

Then the man raises his eyebrows and adds, "You might know him as James. James Scott."

# 30

This entire week I've guessed that something's been up with James, but never anything like this. Now I'm thinking he's right. He does need bodyguards.

"James Scott? Why do you want him?"

The man bares his teeth and warns me, "If I tell you, I'm gonna have to kill you."

Enough said. More than enough. My mind is clicking through everything James told me in the past few days. He's here because his mom is *doing something important.* She *double-crossed* the wrong people. *Not* his dad. She's *testifying.*

Just like the US Marshals' witness Carlos has been transporting.

Holy mother of massive mistakes. I've done it again.

A Mafia family, Gran said. A crime syndicate.

James's mom is the witness. And they want her dead. And they haven't been able to nab her so they're after James, too.

That's what all those Internet posts were about. They were talking about Sydney Brown and the lacrosse team because of James. And this Mob family hired Comcast Man to steal the student records and put up cameras. It was never about parents, or Kyle, or politics.

It's all about finding James so they can stop his mom from testifying against them.

Kyle was always safe—I look over at him—until now. I inhale and face front. Otto is squinting at me, but not in his usual deranged way. It's as if he's about to cry and he doesn't want to.

I never thought I'd feel any sympathy for Otto, but at the moment, I feel very, very sorry for him—for all of us.

"So, you boys are gonna help me out, understand?"

I touch my pocket, wishing I had my phone. "What do you want us to do?"

Mob Guy smirks back at me. "I want you to text your friend James and tell him to meet you in front of the dorm."

"He's at the dorm already. He's getting his—" Kyle stops midsentence, probably realizing he should have kept his mouth shut.

Mob Guy is grinning. "Oh, you're a good rat. I can see I have the right young men for this job."

We need to figure out a way out of this car, away from this psycho, before we all end up at the bottom of a lake.

"I don't have his number in my phone," says Kyle.

The man's forehead squeezes together and he cocks his head. He definitely doesn't buy it. "Try again," he says.

"Listen, sir," I say. "I'm the only one who has James's number."

Mob Guy starts breathing heavy. "I don't care whose phone you use, just text him." Then he shakes his head. "On second thought, call him. On speaker."

I don't want to admit it, but it's gonna come out sooner

or later. "I don't have my phone. I got in trouble and a teacher took it."

Mob Guy is on the verge of hyperventilating and begins to wave his hands theatrically. Under normal circumstances, I don't mind melodramatic people. It's different when they're holding a gun.

We've got to handle this mess one step at a time, 'cause we're not getting anywhere sitting in this limousine. I look out the darkened window as it speeds down some side street. Actually, we are getting somewhere, and that's a problem, too.

I nudge Kyle. "Give me your phone."

He doesn't argue. He reaches into his pocket and presses the side of his phone as he hands it over.

"It's off," he says, almost apologetically. And then I get it. For once he's sorry Kang couldn't track him.

While it's booting up, I close my eyes and picture James's number on my screen. When the keyboard comes up, I press each digit, hoping I've got it right. I'm pretty sure I do; this is where my thing for remembering numbers comes in handy.

Mob Guy narrows his eyes, and they hit me like a heat-seeking missile. I get his message loud and clear and press the speaker on.

"Hello?" It's James.

I don't want to speak. I want to hang up. I do the opposite of both those things. "Hey, James, it's Max."

"Oh, hey. I didn't recognize the number."

"Yeah, uh..." I only pause for a second, but it's enough.

"Hello, Michael. How are you?" Mob Guy's voice rattles its warning.

There's silence on James's end. He knows.

Mob Guy chuckles. "I haven't seen you and your mom since the holiday party. How is she?"

Still silence.

"I have a few of your friends here." He looks at each of us. "Boys, please remind me of your names."

Visions of my grandmother, the president, Special Forces, the army, the marines and the air force all converging on the Sydney Brown campus at once fill my mind. Talk about headlines: CLAYTON STONE CREATES NATIONAL SECURITY EMBARRASSMENT. 12 DEAD, 18 INJURED.

Nope. Kyle can't say his name.

"I'm Max. Otto is beside you, and this is William," I say, pointing to Kyle.

"Michael," says Mob Guy, "I don't want to hurt these nice young men. So do us all a favor and be in front of your dorm building in three minutes. Do not call anyone, or one of these boys will die. And I won't stop until your mother and father are gone, too. Is that understood?"

This time, James answers immediately. "Yes. I'll be there."

Mob Guy reaches across the car and swipes the phone out of my hand. With a quick flick he ends the call and then swats the privacy window. "Back to the dorms. Use the diplomatic ID again."

When he turns back to us, he smiles. "Would any of you like a drink? We have Coke products and iced tea. Not sweetened, I'm afraid. They only do that down south."

Not that I'm thirsty, but what the heck is he talking about? "No thanks," I say.

Otto's eyes are fluttering like he's about to faint, and

Kyle's mouth is hanging open in shock, as if he can't believe this is happening.

Three minutes is closing in on two minutes and I need a plan. But what? Gramps always talked about the "critical path," or figuring out the most important step in a process and doing it first. In this case it probably means putting the most important person first. *Think*, Clayton.

Let's say Otto, Kyle and I walk out of this car. Once Kyle is safe, what do I do? If James willingly gets into this limo to save us, we can't let Mob Guy drive off. Nothing good will happen after that. I've got to figure out a way to stop it from happening.

I stare at the gun, back in Mob Guy's lap. He's relaxed now, looking out the window with a satisfied expression. He's getting exactly what he wants: James.

We're waved through the gate, which is crazy. I guess "diplomats" can go just about anywhere. James is standing at the end of the dorm entrance, waiting, holding his lacrosse stick in one hand.

"Sir," I say, to get Mob Guy's attention as the limo slows down. "Can William have his phone back?"

Mob Guy stares across the vehicle. "Do I look stupid to you?"

"No, sir," I say, shaking my head. I hope Otto and Kyle are paying close attention to what I'm saying. "I'm sure he wouldn't call for help or anything, since that would put James in danger. But the police can track phones when they make calls, right? So I was just thinking you might want to get rid of it."

Mob Guy's face flushes, and I can tell he wants me to shut up. But he can't help talking back to me, either. "By the time they call anybody, we'll be twenty miles away—maybe even in the air."

The limo stops, and the driver gets out. He walks around the back of the vehicle and opens the door, right next to James.

Mob Guy waves his gun at all of us. "Understand one thing. Keep your mouths shut. I get caught, none of you will be safe ever again. Not your families, either." Then he jabs the gun toward Kyle. "You first. Get out."

Kyle looks at me briefly, and I move my eyes sideways. I hope he knows what I'm saying.

"Otto," I say. "Are you okay? You look like you're going to barf."

I don't know whether Otto catches on, or whether he really is about to hurl again, but he follows my cue and leans forward with a long moan.

"Oh, no you don't," says Mob Guy, pulling up Otto's collar and giving him a shove forward. "Not again."

I move to my left, out of Otto's way, as Kyle steps out of the limo, sending me a quick nod as he does. Otto puts his hand on Kyle's back and follows him to fresh air.

"You, stay put," says Mob Guy.

It's funny he says that, 'cause that's exactly what I'm planning to do.

"Tony!" he bellows to the driver. "Get that kid in here."

Next thing I know, James is ducking inside. We lock eyes as he sits beside me.

"No," says Mob Guy, "you by me. And what'd you bring that stick for? Leave it over there."

I take a long breath as James changes places, leaving his stick and the two balls inside the pocket.

Mob Guy puts out his free hand. "Gimme your phone," he says. "But turn it off first."

The front door of the limo closes, and we start to move as James turns off his phone and gives it to Mob Guy.

"Michael, I'm very sorry about all this. I liked your mother. She was a good bookkeeper. The best." He sighs long and loud. "It's really a shame she started working with the feds. You and her coulda had good, long lives."

A chill trickles down my spine like crushed ice. Mob Guy is saying this face-off is over, and he's won the ball.

No doubt it's a bad situation. James is next to a seriously dangerous man who's best friends with his gun, and he and his mom will probably die whether or not she testifies.

And I'm here. Shoot.

Nope. That's the whole point: don't shoot!

Didn't I have a plan two minutes ago? It's hard to remember.

Okay, first, Kyle is safe. Job number one, check.

Number two. Otto is safe. And even though he's been a jerk to me and basically every kid at SB, I'm glad he's okay. Plus, he has his phone, and that is huge right now, because of number three. Which is, Mob Guy still has Kyle's phone, and yes, he ended my phone call with James, but he never turned it off again.

So if Kyle and Otto are thinking clearly, they can get Kang to GPS that thing in twenty seconds or less. Of course, first they have to find Kang and explain everything. And Kang is probably a stomping five shades of ticked off since Kyle ditched him *and* turned off his phone. But the point is, it's on now.

Help could be on its way. Maybe.

So what do I do? And when?

I look past where Mob Guy and James are sitting to the driver. The privacy window is open. I could use a stun pen right now.

Stun. That's a good word.

We need to stun Mob Guy to stop him.

The limo takes a sharp corner as we pull out of the school's dorm entrance onto a real road, and one of the balls escapes James's stick and rolls down the carpet.

Mob Guy is saying something over his shoulder to the driver, and I gesture with my chin to the ball.

James catches my drift and captures it between his shoes. Then he nods at me. Whatever I do, he'll follow through.

We're barreling down a highway at full speed. I have a feeling there will only be one right moment, so we gotta pick it carefully.

Mob Guy digs in the console to his right and brings out what looks like a burner phone. He flips it open and turns it on, snickering to himself.

After a couple of minutes he holds it to his ear. "Doug, how are you?"

I'm listening to every word, hoping for a clue about what's going on as Mob Guy rattles on. "Yeah, get the message to the feds. I want Priscilla to know I got the package. Plus a bonus."

At the mention of Priscilla, James's entire body quivers. That must be his mom.

There's another pause, and Mob Guy grunts and looks at his watch. "Tell Mick we'll be there in less than five. I wanna be in the air fast. You got the takeout from DiAngelo's?"

His face spreads into a gigantic smile. The answer must have been affirmative.

After Mob Guy hangs up, he turns the phone off, puts the window down and chucks it out the window.

A disposable phone is disposable, I guess.

We're heading down a tree-lined road at lightning speed, and all I can think of is the warning my mom used to repeat when she'd talk about stranger danger: *Don't let a bad person take you to a second location. Fight.*

An airplane is definitely a second location. If Kang and Gran or whoever hasn't found us by then, we're crud out of luck. It'll be up to me and James to get ourselves out of this mess.

The limousine cranks left onto a rough gravel road and slows down. We must be getting close.

Suddenly the trees disappear. We're in an open field, and there's a small plane with men posted around it. They're waiting for us.

I've ridden in a lot of planes over my thirteen years, because my grandparents used to take me everywhere with them, but small planes make me sick. If Mob Guy didn't like Otto barfing all over his limo, he's definitely not gonna appreciate me once we take off in that thing. He'll ditch me and the cookies I'm tossing right out the door. Which would be okay if it happened now, in this limo, but at ten thousand feet? Not so much.

My stomach's feeling queasy as we bump our way over the uneven field, and I force myself not to look at the plane. Now I've got one more reason to end this ASAP.

The driver brakes hard and we stop about twenty-five yards from the plane. He immediately gets out of the car, and then Mob Guy starts moving, too, past me and out of the limo. "Stay here," he says to us, with barely a look backward as he slams the door shut.

"Max, what do we do?" James whispers.

"Put that ball in your pocket," I say as I reach down to his stick and put the other one in mine. "And grab anything else—one of those Coke bottles, maybe." I have no idea what I'm saying, but I figure anything will do at this point. "Did you ever get clocked by Coach's radar gun?"

James crumples his forehead. "What?"

"Your shot. How fast are you?"

"Oh," says James, finally understanding. "Pretty fast. Seventy-five miles per hour is my top speed."

Holy mother of burning rubber, I can't touch that. I hand the stick to him and stuff the other ball in my pocket. "Your job is to hit somebody, and hit them good."

"Who? And when?"

I shrug. "I don't know. We have to figure it out as it happens. Just like a game."

James grins back at me. "Yeah, okay. Just like a game."

I listen closely. Something doesn't sound right. It's out of place, beyond the loud conversation going on outside, just a few feet away. A soft knocking, barely audible, is coming from—

"James—er, I mean, Michael?" I say, peering hard out the darkened window. It might be my imagination, but I think I see a line of blurry dots in the sky. "Let's hope those are helicopters and help is here." I turn and look James in the eye. "On my count, we're going to go out this door and run for our lives, okay? Don't stop running, whatever you do."

Now there's yelling and two men are sprinting to get

inside the plane, pointing to the sky. They see the copters, too. I lean to my left, to the door opposite the plane, hoping nobody will see us on this side, and signal to James. The time is now: we've got to escape before it's too late.

I crack the door, praying we get enough of a head start, and then push it wider, stepping out and pressing off the ground, launching myself into the open. I can feel James behind me, but then he calls out.

I turn slightly and see James and the lacrosse stick, caught in the door. I pivot back, grab the stick and twist, setting it and James free. We both take off again, the copters getting louder and closer as their blades beat the air in warning, and I know the mobsters will be seconds behind us.

I hold tight to the lacrosse stick as I run and imagine that it's making me faster. We have to be fast enough.

Still running, I glance back again. My heart sinks.

Mob Guy has caught James, and his arm is slung across James's neck. He doesn't even look for me, he just starts dragging James around the limo and across the field, toward the plane, where the other men are boarding. They don't care about me. Like they didn't care about Otto or Kyle. They only need James.

James sends me a panicked look, but there's something else. He's squirming, and I can tell he's not only resisting, trying to get away, he's struggling for something. He wrenches within Mob Guy's grip one last time and manages to nudge the ball out of his pocket. As it drops to the ground, our eyes meet.

Somehow we both know: that's the game ball.

# 32

I look to the sky, desperate for help. The line of helicopters is growing in size and number, and without a doubt, the good guys are almost here.

My eyes return to James. Mob Guy's dragged him past the limo, and a wave of adrenaline flushes throughout my body, telling me we're not in the middle of a movie. Unfortunately, in real life, sometimes the good guys are too late.

As the helicopters race toward us, I remember what Gramps said about firefighters. *When everybody else is rushing away from a burning building, they're rushing inside—so they can save lives.*

I need to do the same thing. There isn't any other choice. James is my friend, and I'm going to do my best to save him.

I must run as fast as I can into this fire. It might get us both killed, but it's the only chance James has, and it's the only chance his mom has. He's in this mess because his mom is trying to do the right thing: put these mobsters in prison.

And he's also in this mess because I didn't listen to

my gut. I was so busy trying to be Kyle's friend, I wasn't enough of a friend to James.

Michael.

I sprint. James isn't the goal. That monster Mob Guy is.

Not only do I hear the copters, now I feel them in my chest, and again I raise my eyes to the sky. They're coming lower, approaching in a half-circle, and I can feel air start to draft against my face. But they've slowed their descent, because now they see that Mob Guy has James—and they won't close in on that plane if James gets on board.

I keep running. It's up to me to make sure that doesn't happen.

I only have one ball to make this happen. Two, if I can get to the one James dropped.

I pull ball number one from my pants as I go, reach to the end of my stick and tuck it inside the mesh of the pocket. Mob Guy is fighting his way to the airplane steps, but James isn't making it easy for him. He's gone limp, and as Mob Guy drags him, he's lifting each leg and dropping his heels, digging into the ground like a backhoe.

Heaving big gulps of air, his forehead shiny with sweat, Mob Guy is growling mad. He waves his gun in front of James's face and then holds it to his neck.

Mob Guy gets exactly what he wants: our attention. In an instant James stops struggling and I freeze, dead in my tracks.

Satisfied now that he has full control again, Mob Guy continues moving toward the airplane stairway. Except for the limo driver, who's waiting at the bottom of the steps to help get James inside, the other men are already aboard.

When the driver sees me, he takes out *his* gun and aims. At me.

I put my brain on fast forward, thinking, what if—

But then I remember, it's not what if, it's what *is*.

One thing at a time. I can't stop Mob Guy if I'm dead. My shot isn't as fast as James's, but it'll have to do. I check that the ball is still in the pocket. It is.

When I look back, the driver is ready to pull the trigger. I go back to what I told James about acting like we're on the field, in a game.

We *are* on a field, but this is no game. My opponent is that man and his gun, and the bullet he's about to send my way to stop me from helping James.

The wind from the copters is picking up, and the thump of the rotors coming toward us is loud, wop-wop-wopping the air times a thousand, making it almost impossible to concentrate. Except I have to concentrate.

I take a deep breath and sink into the play. Just like Gramps said, the information is always there, I only need to look for it. So I look.

The limo driver's right-handed, and he's leaning to his left—odds are I need to go in the opposite direction. His shoulders rock slightly, and I sidestep to my left, bringing the stick behind me just as he fires. The instant the gun kicks back in his hands, I know the bullet's gonna hit me unless—

With no time to think, I push off the ground and propel myself into the air, whipping the stick forward with all my might. The ball sails past James and Mob Guy, into the driver's chest, knocking him to his knees as I land shoulder-first on the ground.

The driver falls across the steps and drops his gun as sudden strong gusts of dust and wind blow all around us, telling me the first helicopters must be landing. But I don't dare look because this isn't over, and nothing matters until it is. Not even the spasms of pain burning across my shoulder.

My whole left side has gone limp, so I use my good arm to push upright and scour the ground for the ball James dropped, cringing with each move. I force myself to ignore the pain and the whooshing noise of incoming helicopters echoing in the background. Then I see it, a few feet away, but my left arm is basically useless. I grab my stick with my right hand and desperately rake the rippling grass, finally scooping the ball.

The driver is moving, getting to his feet, searching for his gun. And Mob Guy is backing toward the stairs, one arm boomeranged across James's neck and the other waving his gun at me.

I get to my knees and then stand, gripping my stick in my right hand, thankful that Gramps always made me practice with both. I pull my stick back, knowing this is my last shot—and maybe the last thing I do on this earth. Even right-handed, and with no power from my left side, it has to be faster and harder than any ball I've ever thrown, no matter how much—or if—it kills me. James can't get on that plane. If he does, everything his mom has done is lost. He's lost.

I home in on my target and force the stick forward in one furious motion, sending every single last drop of myself with it. The ball fires like a miracle through the wind, strong, tight and fast, and nails Mob Guy square in the forehead. His neck flies back and he releases James as he crumples to the grass: ground zero.

The limo driver reaches out, grasping at James, but then his eyes grow wide as he scans the field beyond us. I turn to see rivers of Special Forces spilling out of the copters that have landed, and they're all running for the airplane—and us.

The driver kicks Mob Guy out of the way and scrambles up the steps, glancing over his shoulder as the stairs begin to pull up behind him. As the stairs retract and the door closes, the plane starts rolling, but there are copters still hovering in the air, finally close enough to block its way. Mob Guy is out cold on the ground, and his plane has nowhere to go.

My heart is thumping fast; the happy ending isn't here yet. And then I see James, shaky and uncertain, inching away from where Mob Guy lies, and my chest heaves in relief. Our eyes connect as we stumble toward each other.

And as the chaos of uniformed officers taking control of Mob Guy and his getaway plane unfolds around us, James and I grip each other in a way only good friends can.

Neither of us speaks, but that's okay. James is alive, and his nightmare is almost over.

There's nowhere to go in the commotion of uniformed soldiers and suits who've surrounded not only the airplane, but the limo and a car parked on the other side of the plane.

James clutches my shoulder and I flinch.

"Are you okay?"

"Yeah, I just fell on it," I say. "But we can't stay here."

James nods, as wary as I am about this video game

combat zone we've found ourselves in. Not counting the lacrosse stick, we're the only ones within a square mile without weapons, and the amount of ammo power on the field tells me the advisable thing to do is dig a hole and hide under a pile of rocks.

"What do we do?" he says.

"First we back up, very, very, slowly, and get out of their way," I say, gesturing to the teams hustling all around us. Next I point to the sky, where three official-looking mega-helicopters are hovering at the far end of the field. "Then we wait for them."

Thursday, May 10, 2:04

# 33

Marine One, the helicopter that carries the president, lands precisely, one copter ahead of it on the ground, while the other waits in the air. Before my goose bumps get going at the thought of POTUS being here, another caravan catches my eye.

A line of vans and SUVs is barreling across the field from the same direction we came from in the limousine earlier. And right up front, leading the pack, a black Suburban storms across the field, practically flying as it bounces over every dirt mound and divot. Without even seeing through the blacked-out windows, I know who's driving: Gran.

The Suburban changes direction as it homes in on James and me, while the vehicles in its wake fan out and scatter around the perimeter of military helicopters.

The Suburban throws up a mix of dust, dirt and grass as it skids to a stop several yards shy of where we stand. All four doors pop open at once.

Sure enough, Gran swoops out of the driver's side door like a tropical bird in her fuchsia blazer. She takes quick long strides and draws her weapon. Captain Thompson appears from out of nowhere, shadowing her every move as they scan the area and move toward us. They are both dressed as themselves; Captain Thompson is even wearing his sling again. I wish he would get better.

At five feet away they abruptly stop, and Gran's eyes sweep the surrounding area one more time. She barks a few orders at the brigade of suits, who have sprouted like mushrooms behind her, telling a few to stand their ground and the others to check in with some colonel.

She slips her gun back into the holster hidden underneath her hot-pink jacket—I guess since we're upright and breathing—and takes a long, relieved breath. That is, until she examines me more closely. Then her eyes narrow, her lips tighten and her face turns the color of chalk.

Gran glares an order: *Stay still!* She then reaches out to examine my shoulder while Captain Thompson observes from behind her, his eyes traveling all the way to my hand. I look down at my dangling arm, and when I look up again, the captain's shaking his head.

Gran presses the insert in her ear and calls for a first-aid kit and the nearest medical team. When I open my mouth to object, she silences me with wide eyes.

After she's done issuing orders that stop just short of calling a surgeon, she continues speaking to James and me as though she really can do her job without being a freaked-out grandmother. I know she can't, but whatever. I hold my arm and try to listen over the sizzling pain I'm not going to admit to.

"Mr. Carrington," she says, gesturing to the advancing

medics. "Let's have these people decide what needs to be done about your shoulder, shall we? Meanwhile, I'd like to express our gratitude. Once more this week, you've managed to help us do our job."

Oh, yeah. It's easy to remember Gran and Captain Thompson *aren't* themselves, or they *are* themselves, because they're right in front of me. But I keep forgetting that I'm *not me.* So what should Max Carrington say to the head of the Special Service? "Er, no problem. Ma'am. Chief Stone."

I guess they think I mean it's no problem to touch me, 'cause one of the medics scissors my shirt halfway off without even saying hello, all while Gran zeroes in on James.

"Michael Basso, I presume?"

James nods. "Yes, ma'am. Um, Chief."

Gran smiles. "It appears that you're all right. You weren't hurt?"

"No, ma'am. Thanks to Max, I'm okay."

I look from James to Gran. "But I think James, er, Michael, is worried about his mom."

"Of course," says Gran apologetically. "Your mother is fine. We have her completely secured, don't we, Captain?" She turns to Captain Thompson, who's kept his mouth shut so far.

He gives a quick nod. "Yes. I can't wait to hear how you two managed to take down one of the biggest Mob bosses on the East Coast, but you've essentially cut the snake off at the head. So I'd say the immediate threat to your mom and you, Michael, is significantly reduced."

Gran lifts her chin. "But that doesn't mean it's nonexistent. So you and your mother both will be staying at the safest safe house possible until she has completed her testimony. As a matter of fact"—Gran's eyes momentarily flit to the helicopters at the far end of the field—"someone is waiting to escort you. There's only one problem."

James grabs my good arm—the right one.

"What's the problem, Chief Stone?" he asks.

"Well, it's not such a huge problem." Gran chuckles. "It's only that you'll have to flip a coin to see who gets the Lincoln Bedroom. Your mother is being quite stubborn about it."

Just beyond Gran there's an incoming line of agents—the president's detail. Gran turns like she's been expecting them. "Take good care of this young person, gentlemen. Tell President Hampton we'll be checking on Michael and his mother later."

I shiver. Probably because the medics are still working on my shoulder, spraying cold goop on me and stuff. Not because this whole thing with James and Kyle is almost over.

I look from the president's men to James, and then back at my grandmother and the captain. "You mean, er, Michael has to leave now? He's not coming back to school?"

Gran begins to answer, but then another convoy of black vehicles appears out of the line of trees. "Speaking of school," she says finally, "I should mention that your friends were extremely worried about you two and made quite a commotion in the halls of Sydney Brown." She pauses and then chuckles. "Poor Agent Kang. Kyle, Otto and Amber bullied the stuffing out of him, insisting we employ every possible effort to rescue you. He of course told them a nuclear missile would be out of the question, but barring that"—she extends her arms to the field of military helicopters, armed forces and special agents commandeering the plane, car and field, and rounding up the mobsters—"we spared nothing."

"*Otto?*" James and I say together as the first SUV in the line pulls up and parks even closer to us than Gran did.

"Yes," says Gran. "Otto Penrod *the Third*."

I stare at James, who looks just as shocked as I feel.

Two suits exit the Suburban and march toward Gran like they're on a mission. One of them is Agent Kang.

"Agent Kang, how may I help you?" says Gran.

"Chief Stone, I'm here on behalf of Kyle Hampton and the students of Sydney Brown. They are very concerned about Max and James and would appreciate a full update as soon as possible." He briefly tilts his head at us. "Preferably in person."

I can hardly believe that many words came out of Agent Kang's mouth at once; he almost sounds like a person. Maybe he can answer a question.

"Do you know what happened with the debate?"

Agent Kang pivots on his heels and faces me. "The debate was delayed because the students put *themselves* in lockdown inside the auditorium. All one hundred eighty students have refused to do anything until they receive word that you and James are safe."

A weird tingle travels down my spine and I want to speak, but I can't.

Gran responds for me. "Is that so?" she says. "Headmistress Williams must be quite beside herself."

"That is correct," says Agent Kang, turning back to her.

"Do you think it would be possible for me to escort these two young men back to Sydney Brown, Chief Stone? I'm not sure I want to return without them."

Gran lifts her chin. "It would mean keeping the president waiting." Her eyes dart back to James and me. "What do you boys think?"

The corner of James's mouth rises slightly. "Headmistress Williams obviously needs our help."

"I agree—a hundred eighty is a lot of kids," I say. "It's practically our duty."

Gran swirls full circle to the waiting presidential detail behind her. "Gentlemen, I will see to it that Michael is transported to the White House. Tell the president to call me, or his son, if he has any questions."

The special agent in charge nods and gives an order, and then they all about-face. In less than sixty seconds they're a blur, almost back to Marine One.

Gran steps toward the medic in charge. "How is this young man?" she says, with a quick look at me.

The officer stands at attention as he answers. "I don't think it's broken, Chief; looks like a minor separation of the shoulder. We gave him something for the pain. Besides that, ice and rest should do it."

Gran nods. "Thank you. You're dismissed."

She looks and sounds all formal, but I know that on the inside she's letting out a huge sigh of relief and probably doing some sort of grandmother jig. I also know she knows that with all the bullets flying, it could've been a lot worse.

Still playing the chief, Gran returns her attention to Agent Kang. "Captain Thompson and I need to wrap things up here. I'll be at the school to pick both boys up as soon as we're finished. I'd appreciate it if you'd stick with them until then. We should debrief Max as soon as possible." Then she sneaks a wink at me. "I'll call his father and let him know."

"Yes, Chief," Agent Kang says.

"Very well, you may go," she says. "But Max, I'd like a word with you before you join them."

James and Agent Kang head to the Suburban, and Gran signals to Captain Thompson.

"How does it feel, Max?" she says as the captain steps closer.

"It's fine," I say. Not quite the truth, but if I say anything else, she'll be strapping me to my bed until next week. Hopefully the Tylenol will kick in and I'll be good as new by tomorrow morning, just like the medic promised.

Captain Thompson laughs. "He'll be fine, Liza." Then he meets my eyes and lowers his voice. "But Clayton, I'm sorry. This was my fault. If I had dug deeper when James showed up, none of this would have happened." He raises his right hand and with an awkward tug, pulls his sling off. Then he lifts it over my head and fiddles with it until it fits.

"Welcome to the injured-in-the-line-of-duty club, my boy," he says when he's done. "You did good work, and I'm proud of you."

"We both are, Clayton." Gran lets out a long breath. "Now get out of here. I'll call the headmistress and have her meet you and Michael with some clean shirts. I'm certain she doesn't want you traipsing around SB looking like *that*."

I know she wants to hug me, and maybe Captain

Thompson does, too. Only, since I'm still Max, they can't. And this is not the time to get all huggy, anyway, with the messed-up shirt and all.

"Okay, sure," I say. I start toward the Suburban, then have an idea. "Hey, Captain, since it's a club, we should pick up some burgers at Big Stone's tonight and go visit Carlos in the hospital. Sort of celebrate that everybody's alive. We all *were* sort of working on the same case; me with James, and Carlos with James's mom—and you with me."

Gran and Captain Thompson exchange doubtful glances, back to business mode. "We have work to do, young man," says Gran.

"No problem," I say over my shoulder. "You can debrief me on the way to the hospital. That's your job, right?"

And before either of them can respond, I open the back door of the Suburban and step inside, because Gran's right. There's still work to do.

And that's precisely why I'm heading to Sydney Brown.

# 34

Kang doesn't talk much on the way to the school, and James and I are pretty quiet, too. I wonder about a lot of things as we drive, like, should I start calling James Michael, or will he keep the name James? Or will he need to change his identity again? Maybe by next week he'll be a Rod, or a Spencer, or maybe he'll go completely crazy and call himself Otto.

I think back to the fake names I've had since I started working for the Special Service: Billy, Finn and now Max. And the list will probably get longer. Who knows who I'll be tomorrow, next week or next month?

The Suburban pulls up to the school entrance, and as James and I head up the walkway we pass an easel holding a giant poster, advertising the debate: Stars vs. Stripes. Amber keeps saying the issues that Monique and Peter talk about are more important than which party they represent.

Mascots. Symbols. Names. The Special Service can change me from a Clayton to a Leopold if they want. But that won't change who I am and what's important to me. Like Kyle can bounce around from the Stars to the Stripes no matter what his dad thinks. He takes his own ideas with him. And it was the same when I came to SB and had to face off against my Masters teammates. I did that as myself, even though my name was Max.

Kang and his men flank James and me as we head to the auditorium. It's weird—this is probably the last time I'll walk these halls, since my job here is basically over. But that's not what's bothering me.

I grip the door handle that will take us into the auditorium and I meet James's eyes, knowing that soon we'll have to say good-bye. And it'll probably be forever.

"Ready?"

"I guess," he says. And the way he says it, I think he's feeling a little sorry, too. Just like me.

We enter the auditorium together. The seats are overflowing, kids draped over them, backward and frontways, and there are circles of small groups in the aisles and all over the stage. They don't notice James and me at first. It's the giant Kang and the rest of his posse that get their attention as the agents lumber down the aisle behind us.

The bustling and chatter quickly taper off as the students realize we've made it, and all eyes converge on us. I hear a few comments about my sling and the condition of our uniforms, which I guess makes sense. I've lost my bow tie, and my tucked-in shirt is gaping down the middle, and James looks like he blew through a dust storm.

But it's too late to drop by Headmistress Williams's office for those replacement shirts, so we keep moving fast toward the front, where Kyle and Amber are standing together on the stage's stairs. As we approach, I reach behind and grab James, pulling him forward.

Kyle and Amber step toward us, their arms out wide, and bring us up to the stage. They pull us in for a big group hug, and the auditorium instantly echoes with cheers and applause. Seconds later, Peter and Monique appear from behind, their arms stretching around us, too.

In the middle of the cheering, I look over Kyle's shoulder, and the last person I expect is standing just outside the circle, watching. I don't know what happened to Otto; besides the fact that he's wearing a vomit-free shirt, his whole face is different.

Gramps used to say *A leopard can't change his spots*. And that might be true, at least on the outside. But as Otto steps even closer, he puts his long arms around Kyle and Amber and Peter, and he looks at James, and then at me, and smiles. Could it be possible? Is Otto changing his stripes from the inside? 'Cause in this moment, it doesn't seem like he wants to hurt Kyle, or Peter, or James or anybody.

"Hey," I say, over all the laughing and good kind of school chatter. "Aren't we going to have a debate?"

Otto immediately drops back and turns to Monique and with a grand gesture offers his arm to her. Then he cocks his head toward Peter and gives a quick signal for him to follow.

Just as quickly as the celebration started, it stops. And the whole school watches in silence as Otto Penrod the Third escorts Monique to the closest podium, shakes her hand and then walks Peter to the other.

Otto leans over to the microphone and looks first at James, Kyle and me on the stage, next to Monique and Peter, and then out at the students packed in the audience.

"I just want to say that I've been a colossal jerk, and I

almost ruined this election. I've never had to say I'm sorry for anything in my life." Otto's eyes find me and James and Kyle again. "But today I'm really glad I'm alive to say, I *am* sorry."

Otto turns and holds his hand out to Peter. And when they shake, I know, we all know, democracy is back in play at Sydney Brown.

The debate is in full swing, with Monique and Peter going back and forth about whether money should be equally distributed among the boys' and girls' teams, no matter which of those teams brings in more dollars.

Everybody is paying attention, heads swinging back and forth like it's a tennis match.

I keep changing my mind about who's winning the argument; then Headmistress Williams taps my shoulder and whispers for me to follow her into the atrium.

Outside the auditorium, she gestures for me to follow her down the hallway. "I'm sorry to interrupt, Max, but Chief Stone is coming to collect you and James in a few minutes, and she wanted me to make sure you'd be ready." She reaches into her pocket as we walk and adds, "Also, Ms. Miller wanted me to return your phone."

"Thank you, ma'am," I say, taking the SpiPhone and tucking it in my pocket.

"Of course," she says. "I told Chief Stone we'd meet her here. She wants to speak with you privately."

I hear a familiar click-clack of heels and look ahead to see a woman wearing a bright pink jacket heading our way.

"There she is now. I need to get back to the debate. Please tell Chief Stone I'll send James up in a few minutes."

"Yes, ma'am, I will," I say.

I watch the headmistress leave and then turn to wait for Gran. She's walking fast, with a huge stack of binders in her arms. That's not good.

I want to go back to Masters. It's where my lifelong friends are, and it's where I belong. The question is how to stop thinking about Laci when Toby likes her so much. And there's another problem.

I stare at the binders as Gran gets closer. "You're going to tell me about how much homework I've got to make up, right?"

"Oh, Clayton, I'm not worried about that right now," Gran says, catching her breath. "We can take care of that in summer school, while you're at the Special Service Training Academy. Right now we need to get you ready for your next assignment." Gran pauses and looks me up and down.

"I know you're barely thirteen, Clayton, but do you think you can pull off fifteen? Just for the weekend?"

"Uh, I guess. Maybe," I say. "Why?"

"Because there's a young lady in town from Bulgaria, and she needs a date to a ball."

Holy mother of undercover!

I'm in.

# ACKNOWLEDGMENTS

I would not have been able to write *Clayton Stone, Facing Off* without the enthusiasm and support of my editor at Holiday House, Sally Morgridge. Beyond her top-notch editing skills and advice, her fondness for Clayton and his supporting cast warms my heart. I feel fortunate to work with Sally, and thankful to her and the rest of the Holiday House staff for their help in bringing my junior undercover agent to life again!

I am also grateful to my agent, Ginger Knowlton, who, in any circumstance, always knows exactly what to say. I rest easy knowing that Ginger and the team at Curtis Brown are taking care of me.

There are no words to appropriately thank my talented critique partner, writing confidante and friend, Rebecca Barnhouse, who insists I'm funny (no matter what my family says), and without whom I'd have stopped writing at least a thousand times last week.

I'm also indebted to my extended "writing family," which stretches across the US and even into Canada. Especially, Rose Green, Cyndi Marko and Katie Kennedy, and my SCBWI Blueboard buds, who are always willing to pitch in and brainstorm whenever I'm faced with an earth-shattering problem and my mind is blank.

A deep-in-the-shadows thank-you to my own "undercover" agent, who knows exactly how they helped me but wishes to remain anonymous, because, duh, they are "undercover."

A special thanks to Holiday House art director Kerry Martin, who designed a book jacket that perfectly captures the essence of Clayton, and to copy editor Barbara Perris, whose legendary skills helped usher both Clayton Stone novels into the world.

Much love and a huge shout-out to my cheerleading cousins, Heather Coryell, Mary Ellen Fleming and Adria Frie; my parents-in-law, Robert Jones, Barbara Jones and Richard Ashwick; and the many friends and family members who reassure and inspire me along the way.

And finally, for their constant encouragement and understanding, I thank my husband, Jeff, and our children, Blake, Kevin, Ena Marie and Thomas. Writing a book wouldn't be half as much fun without their joyful and mischievous presence in my life.